Makepeace, followed ░░░░░░░░░░░░░░
the house. But ju░░░░░░░░░░░░░░
doorway Thornton ░░░░░░░░░░░░░░
her neck and pulled░░░░░░░░░░░░░
the same time there was a distinct *click* and the
next thing she knew Thornton was holding a
switch-blade to her throat . . .

Dempsey had drawn his .44 but it was too late.
He froze, the gun wavering in his hand.

'Drop it, you mother, or I give this doll here an
extra pussy!' cried Thornton.

Dempsey dropped the gun . . .

Also available from Futura

JOHN RAYMOND

DEMPSEY AND MAKEPEACE:

Lucky Streak

Based on the original screenplays by
Dave Humphries and Jesse Carr-Martindale

Futura

A Futura Book

Series created by Golden Eagle Films
Novelization copyright © John Raymond 1985

First published in Great Britain in 1985 by
Futura Publications,
a Division of Macdonald & Co (Publishers) Ltd
London & Sydney

ISBN 0 7088 2735 7

Typeset, printed and bound in Great Britain by
Hazell Watson & Viney Limited,
Member of the BPCC Group,
Aylesbury, Bucks

Futura Publications
A Division of
Macdonald & Co (Publishers) Ltd
Maxwell House
74 Worship Street
London EC2A 2EN
A BPCC plc Company

MAY 22 1992

CHAPTER ONE

The atmosphere in the casino was deceptively placid but James Dempsey was aware of the underlying, latent tension. It was like an electric current running from player to player, making the air tingle. Such a tension is always present in situations where big money is at stake and Dempsey knew that despite the outwardly calm faces around him the stakes were very high indeed. Fortunes were literally being won and lost in that quiet room.

But not, however, at his table. The blackjack game he was playing had a maximum bet of only twenty pounds. It was the casino's equivalent of the shallow end of the pool but Dempsey was content to just paddle around. The deep water was tempting but he knew that's where the sharks were waiting.

The dealer, an attractive girl in a low-cut, black evening dress, dealt out the cards to both him and the only other player at the table. Dempsey looked at his two cards. A king and a ten. He shook his head at the girl. The other player, a middle-aged Chinese man, took another card and stood with the three cards.

The girl then dealt two cards to herself. She had a knave and an eight. She stood, and said, 'Paying nineteen, twenty and twenty-one.' She had a clear, pleasant voice with an accent that Dempsey had come to recognize as upper-middle class.

The Chinese muttered something under his breath and pushed his cards back across the green baize. Dempsey revealed his twenty-one. The girl rewarded him with a brief smile that was near enough to the genuine article not to matter and a twenty pound chip. Dempsey added the latter to the growing pile in front of him. He let his twenty pound bet ride for the next play and won again, this time standing on a pair of queens.

'Looks like your night, Mr Dempsey,' said a voice beside him. 'What's your secret?'

Dempsey glanced round and saw Peter Ferris, the casino manager. Ferris was a smooth and urbane-looking man in his early forties. Dempsey liked him, having detected a real and friendly human being beneath the professional façade.

'No secret. Just clean living,' Dempsey told him.

Ferris made a pained face. 'If clean living ever catches on I'll be out of a job so please don't spread it around.'

Dempsey smiled. 'Doesn't look as if you've got any cause to worry. The joint is really jumping tonight . . .'

The casino was indeed crowded. Arabs, as usual, made up the majority of the gamblers but there were also many Chinese, Greeks, Americans and even a fair number of English.

'I have to admit business isn't bad,' conceded Ferris. 'If only I could figure out a way of stopping you punters from occasionally winning.'

Dempsey laughed and gestured at his pile of chips. 'You let small fry like me clean up a little just to prime the pump.'

'Ah, if only that was the case,' said Ferris. 'Unfortunately we've had some big winners in here during the last couple of weeks. Speaking of which, here comes one of the biggest now . . .'

He nodded towards the lobby. Dempsey turned and saw an imposing Arab in his mid-fifties, and wearing the full traditional regalia, coming in through the casino entrance. He was closely followed by a heavily built European man who had 'bodyguard' written all over him.

'Prince Razul,' explained Ferris to Dempsey as he

beckoned his pit boss, Nick Colino, over. Colino, a sharp-eyed Italian, hurried across.

'Nick, you'd better give Roz another fifty thousand in the float. The Prince always plays her table first,' Ferris told him.

As the pit boss hurried off to comply, Ferris murmured, 'Excuse me, Mr Dempsey,' and moved forward to greet the Arab prince as he emerged from the lobby.

'Good evening, sir . . . very nice to see you with us again.'

Prince Razul flashed the latest in Western dental technology at Ferris and said, 'If my visit tonight is anything like as lucrative as my last one then the pleasure is all mine, Mr Ferris. I trust my usual stakes will be agreeable to you?'

'Of course – the House is happy to accommodate you, sir.'

'I shall play the cards first, I think. Later, perhaps, some roulette . . .'

'Of course, sir,' said Ferris, accompanying him to the blackjack table next to Dempsey's where the stakes were considerably higher. As the Prince seated himself his bodyguard went to the cashier's booth – an elegantly armoured structure standing in the centre of the lobby – and began doling out wads of notes from a briefcase to the tough-looking cashier behind the security glass.

The cashier swiftly counted the notes then said, 'One hundred thousand pounds, Mr Crane.'

'Right on the button,' agreed the bodyguard and started replenishing the briefcase with the stack of chips that the cashier was sliding out under the glass. When he had them all he snapped the briefcase shut and went to join his employer at the blackjack table.

Dempsey watched as the man created an impressive pile of chips in front of the Prince and then faded

7

discreetly into the background. The Prince made his first bet. Dempsey saw, from the colour of the chips, it was at least five hundred pounds. He sighed and returned his attention to his own table.

A few minutes later his concentration was broken by a sudden commotion at the Prince's table. He turned and saw a young, fair-haired man rise unsteadily to his feet. He was shouting at the croupier – another attractive girl dressed in black.

'I tell you that was my card! You dealt him my card out of turn, you stupid tart!'

Wearing a fixed smile the girl murmured something in a soothing tone but he refused to be calmed down.

'Don't argue with me, bitch!' he yelled, his face going dark red with anger. 'I've got eyes in my bloody head! I saw you do it, you brainless slag!'

By this time both Nick Colino and Ferris were converging on him. Colino reached him first. 'What seems to be the trouble, sir?'

'The trouble is your dozy bloody croupier here! Can't deal the bloody cards properly. Why can't you hire people with a bit of intelligence instead of these working-class cretins?'

'I'm sure everything can be sorted out, Mr Bessel,' said Ferris calmly. 'Why don't you come to the bar with me for a drink and we'll have a quiet chat about it.'

Bessel's reaction was to turn and send the cards and chips scattering off the table with a sweep of his arm. 'Fuck your drink and fuck you all!' he yelled.

The pit boss immediately grabbed him from behind, pinioning his arms. Bessel began to struggle violently, lashing out with his feet. A chair toppled with a crash and Prince Razul had to get up hurriedly and move out of the way to avoid being kicked.

Ferris then grabbed Bessel as well and helped the pit boss hustle him away from the table and towards the lobby. Bessel didn't go easily, fighting and yelling every inch of the way.

As the three struggling figures entered the lobby Dempsey heard Prince Razul say with annoyance, 'They seem to be letting just anyone into this establishment nowadays ... if he cannot lose well, why does he gamble?'

Dempsey mused that, unlike the Prince, the young man probably didn't have a couple of oil wells to fall back on.

The struggle had reached the entrance now, with two of the outside doormen hurrying inside to lend assistance. A dinner-suited security man, in the act of collecting several money-bags from the cashier's booth, plainly wanted to join in but didn't dare risk it. Instead he picked up the bags and, still watching the mêlée at the entrance, walked reluctantly back to the open security door that led off from the lobby.

Bessel and his struggling escort finally disappeared through the entrance. For a short time Dempsey could still hear him shouting abuse but then his voice faded into the distance. Ferris was the first to return. He came back into the lobby adjusting his tie and looking flushed from all the exertion. Dempsey felt sorry for him. It seemed a cushy job, being a casino manager, but in reality it was a tough one.

Ferris first hurried over to Prince Razul and began to apologize for the disturbance. The Prince, who had just won heavily on the last play, waved a dismissive hand.

With the Prince mollified Ferris moved among his other, less important, customers murmuring his apologies. When he finally got to Dempsey he seemed to gratefully drop the professional mask. 'Shit,' he muttered, 'what a night. I've got to get in another line of business ...'

'Who was that guy?' Dempsey asked him.

'Jamie Bessel. The son of one of our more privileged families. Born with a silver spoon up his arse and all that. A spoilt, arrogant little bastard as well. Hard to believe he's an ex-Guards captain but he was.'

'One of your regulars?'

'Yes, unfortunately. I'd love to bar him but he has too many connections. I'll probably end up getting some stick for tonight's little fracas.'

'You mean for throwing him out?' asked Dempsey, surprised. 'But what else could you do?'

'Nothing,' admitted Ferris with a shrug. 'But his lot stick together. His friends no doubt have the same opinion of him as I do but they'll automatically take his side. You're an American, Mr Dempsey, so you probably don't know much about our upper classes.'

Dempsey, thinking of Makepeace, smiled wryly and said, 'Well, I know a *little* about them.'

'Then you'll know they form a very exclusive club. The most exclusive in the world. You can only get into it if you're born into it and then you're in it for life, no matter what you do.'

'Sounds to me you don't think too highly of them.'

'That's because I see too much of them in this game. I wasn't completely joking when I said I wanted to get into a different line of business.'

'Then why don't you?'

Ferris smiled guiltily. 'Money, of course, Mr Dempsey. This job pays too well and I have a wife and a mistress to support as well as an eight-year-old daughter. All three of them have expensive tastes.'

Dempsey laughed. 'Sounds like you're well and truly trapped, Peter.'

'I guess so, Mr Dempsey. I guess so,' he said sadly.

'Hey, call me James. Save the formalities for your rich customers.'

Ferris grinned. 'Okay, *James*,' he said. Then, 'You know, you've never mentioned what your line of work is.'

10

'I'm a sort of trouble-shooter. For an oil company,' Dempsey said. He didn't like lying to him but he knew from experience that telling people he was a cop was a good way of stopping a friendly relationship in its tracks. Nor did he think Ferris would believe that he visited the casino merely for his own amusement if he told him the truth.

'Sounds exciting,' said Ferris, a shade wistfully. Then he patted Dempsey on the shoulder and said, 'Well, back to the grindstone. Keep winning, James. The owners can certainly afford it.'

'I'll sure try,' laughed Dempsey. He watched Ferris head off across the casino, the professional, smooth smile back on his face, then turned and nodded to the croupier that he was back in the game.

He was just examining his two cards and wondering whether to stand on a ten and a seven when he looked up and noticed that the girl was frowning slightly at something behind him.

Puzzled, he turned and saw the security man he'd spotted earlier in the lobby coming towards him. The man, in his twenties, was walking oddly, as if he was drunk but trying very hard not to show it. He was holding himself unusually straight and had his right hand clamped inside his dinner jacket.

For a moment Dempsey thought the man was looking straight at him but then he saw that his eyes were unfocused, as if he was deep in concentration.

As the security man continued his approach Dempsey felt a prickle of unease on the back of his neck. Something was wrong, but what . . .?

The man came to a stop about a yard from Dempsey and opened his mouth as if to speak . . .

But instead of words it was a rush of bright red arterial blood that emerged from between his lips. It poured down over the front of his ruffled shirt and black dinner jacket. Then he started to fall.

The croupier screamed.

11

Dempsey stood up but before he could catch him the security guard fell face down across the kidney-shaped blackjack table, his blood splattering over the green baize and the cards.

CHAPTER TWO

'You were doing what?' asked Spikings in a dangerous tone of voice.

'I said I was playing cards. Blackjack. You got an international agreement that says I can't play cards?'

'No, but I'll soon get one if people are going to get shot while you're doing it! What's this going to look like to the top brass at the Yard? "Your man was very quick off the mark, Spikings," they'll say. And I'll have to say, "He was in there playing cards when it was all going on around him." '

They were sitting in the rear of Spikings' car which was parked a short distance from the casino entrance in Charles Street. Three other police cars and an ambulance were also parked there. Despite the late hour a sizable crowd of onlookers had gathered in the narrow Mayfair street, most of them in evening clothes.

'Nothing went on "around me", sir,' said Dempsey stiffly. 'It all happened off-stage. No sound of gun-shots or anything. First thing I knew of it was when this guy practically falls dead on top of me.'

Spikings eyed Dempsey's blood-flecked dinner suit with distaste. 'Don't suppose he had time to tell you who shot him while he was bleeding to death all over you?'

With a touch of annoyance Dempsey said, 'He couldn't talk, sir. One of the bullets must have gone through a lung. He was drowning in his own blood.'

'And you didn't see anything at all?'

'Not a thing.'

'Bugger me,' muttered Spikings. 'Four hundred thousand pounds gets nicked and a security guard gets shot to death and my man on the spot doesn't see a bloody thing. I'll need ear-plugs to block out the sound of all the laughter when they read my report of this at the Yard. I hope you won at your damned game of cards. You'll need to have got *something* out of this mess.'

'Yeah, I did win.'

'I'm overjoyed,' Spikings said sourly. 'I'm so over-joyed I'm gonna let you go drag Makepeace out of bed. You'll like that, I know. I want to see you both in my office within an hour.'

'Yessir.' The thought of disturbing Makepeace's beauty sleep *did* appeal to him. He was about to open the car door when Spikings stopped him with, 'Hang on, Dempsey. One question before you go . . .'

'Yeah?'

'How the hell can you afford to gamble in a place like that on the salary you get?'

Dempsey looked embarrassed. 'My mother, sir,' he mumbled.

'What?'

'My mother. Her second husband left her well set-up and she kind of insists on sending me money. I tell her not to but . . .' He shrugged.

'Great,' growled Spikings. 'Something else to put on my report – my man on the spot was in the casino spending his allowance from his Mum . . . bugger me,' he shook his head with dismay. Then, 'Get moving, Dempsey. And on the way you might as well pick up breakfast for Makepeace. You look like a bloody waiter in that lot . . .'

Makepeace groaned as the doorbell's insistent buzzing hauled her up from the exquisite oblivion of deep, dreamless sleep.

She opened her eyes and fumbled for the clock on her bedside table. Its luminous display told her it was a quarter to three.

'Oh, don't be ridiculous . . .' she muttered. But the doorbell kept buzzing, forcing her to come fully awake. She pushed back the covers and, naked, got out of bed. She grabbed a robe from a nearby chair and put it on as she walked out into the hallway.

At the front door she peered out through the security eyehole and saw, to her dismay, that it was Dempsey standing out there in the corridor. Reluctantly she unchained the door and opened it. Dempsey grinned at her.

'Hi, princess. It's your knight in shining armour. I've come to take you away from all this wealth and privilege . . .'

'First, how did you get past the night-porter downstairs, and secondly, why are you dressed as a waiter?' she asked coldly.

Dempsey winced. 'I used my charm on the night-porter, plus my I.D., and I am *not* dressed as a waiter. These are my playtime clothes.'

She regarded him critically. 'Must get rough in your playground. You've got blood all over you.'

'Relax, princess. It's not my blood.'

'I'm not *un*relaxed. But whose blood is it then?'

'Guy who works at a casino. Or rather he *did*. He's dead and four hundred grand has gone missing. Which is why the Chief wants us both in his office in half an hour.'

'Spikings? At this hour of the morning? Go away, Dempsey, or it *will* be your blood on your waiter's uniform.'

Dempsey glanced at his watch. 'Twenty-nine minutes to go. You coming dressed like that or are you going to put on something less comfortable?' He gestured at her clinging silk gown.

She sighed and held open the door. 'Come in, Dempsey.'

'I thought you'd never ask,' he said as he stepped inside, taking pains to brush against her as he did so.

He ran an admiring eye up and down her body as she shut the door and led the way down the hallway. 'Well, well, I'd never have guessed it . . .'

'Guessed what?' she asked brusquely as she ushered him into the living room.

'You sleep in the raw,' he told her with a grin. 'For some reason I always pictured you as a flannel night-gown and woolly socks type.'

She folded her arms over her chest and glared at him. 'You'll *keep* picturing me in a flannel nightgown if you know what's good for you, Dempsey.'

'Sure, princess, anything you say,' he said placatingly. Then he looked around the room, taking in the obviously expensive but tasteful furnishings. 'Hey, this is some pad you've got here. How come you've never invited me before?'

'I didn't invite you *this* time. You just came.'

Dempsey walked over to an alcove in which a number of sculptured glass objects were displayed on a series of shelves. 'What's with the collection of glass paperweights?' he asked, picking up a ruby-coloured eagle's head.

'They're not paperweights, they're Lalique originals,' said Makepeace. 'And please put that down. It's very valuable. They all are.'

He obeyed. 'Better get a move on, princess. The Chief is not in a good mood.'

Makepeace opened the door to her bedroom and hesitated, a frown on her face as she looked at him. 'I'll be ready in less than a minute. Can I trust you not to destroy an expensive work of art in that time?'

'Hey, princess, you make me sound like some sort of cave man,' he said in a pained voice.

'You *are* some sort of cave man.'

'Look, if it'll make you feel better I'll wait in the bedroom with you.'

'No, it would not make me feel any better. On the

16

contrary, it would make me feel considerably worse. Stay right where you are.'

She disappeared into her bedroom, leaving the door slightly ajar so that they could carry on talking. 'So what's it all about, Dempsey?' she called. 'What have you been up to now?'

Dempsey, his eyes on the gap in the doorway, meandered across the room. Makepeace had taken care to move out of sight but had overlooked a mirror on her open wardrobe door and he was rewarded with a clear side-view of her as she slipped out of the robe.

God, he said to himself, Sergeant Makepeace, you are what I call high-class material . . . Aloud he said, as casually as possible, 'I was just an innocent bystander . . . I go to a casino for a little innocent blackjack, I win a little money with my usual consummate skill, and then suddenly a security guard drops dead on top of my cards.'

'You mean that's all you saw? Just a falling body?' asked Makepeace.

He watched out of the corner of his eye as she climbed into a pair of black lace panties. 'Yeah,' he said wistfully. 'Just a body . . .' His voice trailed away.

'You didn't see the robbers?'

'No one did. The guy was taking the cash upstairs to put in the safe when he was hit.'

'But how did they get away? You can't just walk in and out of those places.'

'I know you can't. And there's nothing wrong with the security at that place. But no one saw anyone come in or leave.'

Seeing that Makepeace had almost finished dressing Dempsey turned his back to the door and then said, 'Hey, are you ready yet?'

'Just about,' she replied. She came out of the bedroom brushing her hair. She was now wearing a white blouse and black skirt. Dempsey turned and gave her an appreciative whistle.

17

Makepeace raised a cool eyebrow at him. 'Doesn't your libido ever take time off?'

'Never when you're around, princess.'

'You sure you wouldn't like a cold shower before we leave?'

'Is that an invitation?'

'I meant by yourself.'

He shook his head sadly. 'Harry, when are you going to come clean and admit to yourself you're secretly crazy about me?'

'Dempsey, the day I do that will be the day I discover I have senile dementia.'

'It's okay, I can wait.'

Makepeace groaned.

James Bessel couldn't keep his eyes off the large, black leather travelling bag sitting beside him on the rear seat of the taxi. There was a smirk on his face and he had to fight the urge to laugh out loud. It wouldn't do to arouse the curiosity of the driver.

But he couldn't resist unzipping the bag part of the way to reveal some of the thick bundles of banknotes.

Resting on top of the money was a .38 Smith & Wesson revolver with an attached silencer.

Bessel smiled lovingly at the money, zipped the bag shut and settled back in his seat with a contented sigh.

CHAPTER THREE

Spikings regarded the file in front of him as if it was a personal enemy. 'Two .38 calibre bullets, probably from a Smith & Wesson,' he read aloud in a grim voice. 'Markings suggested a silencer . . .' He looked up and gave Dempsey a withering glance. 'You might have been blind but at least you weren't going deaf on us as well . . .'

Before Dempsey could protest Spikings went on reading the file. 'The cashier saw the guard go back in, but that's about all he did see – none of the alarm systems upstairs were triggered so we can assume he didn't do a Father Christmas. Whatever he did was neat and fast . . .' He looked up at Dempsey again. '. . . And right under *your* nose, copper.'

Sounding aggrieved, Dempsey said, 'Who am I supposed to be? Superman? I don't have super-hearing. Just as I can't hear penguins farting in Antarctica from here in your office I can't hear people being shot with silenced guns when I'm in the middle of a crowded casino. I'm only human!'

'We've only got your word for that, haven't we, Dempsey?' growled Spikings. 'Personally I have my doubts . . .'

Makepeace quickly stepped in with, 'What about that fight that broke out? Odd, wasn't it, that it almost coincided exactly with the robbery? Could it have been a deliberate ploy? A distraction . . .?'

'Yeah, it's possible,' admitted Dempsey. 'Wouldn't have got the robbers in through the front entrance but I guess someone could have slipped into the passage-way behind the security door while the guard was picking up the cash. But that would mean Bessel himself was involved . . .'

'And that's highly unlikely,' said Spikings, looking at the file again. 'James Spencer Bessel – the family owns half of Wiltshire and quarter of Scotland, not to mention assorted chunks of South Africa, Canada and Australia. What's he want to rob a casino for? Fun?'

Dempsey shrugged. 'Sport, maybe? You know how loony your upper classes are. Look at this one, for example . . .' he gestured at Makepeace.

She glared at him. 'Loony? You can talk – you refugee from the land that's given the world yo-yos, hula hoops and *Dallas*.'

'All right, knock it off you two,' ordered Spikings. 'Anyone would think the pair of you were married the way you carry on.'

Makepeace looked shocked. *'Wha* . . .?' she began angrily.

Spikings held up a hand to silence her. 'Save it, Harry, we've got work to do. Now rolling in money or not, this Bessel character will have to be checked out.'

'Shall we bring him in for questioning?' asked Dempsey.

'Lord, no!' cried Spikings. 'I want him handled with kid gloves. Same goes for the other guests at the casino. Bessel's is not the only well-connected name on the membership list. Half of this mob have got diplomatic immunity so we're instructed to play this a trifle discreetly. Get my drift?'

Makepeace said sourly, 'Yes. You mean when we find the killers we give them a lift to the nearest airport and assist them with their luggage.'

Spikings gave her an icy smile. 'I mean what I said. You play it *discreet*, that's all. Prince Razul, for example, is a very big nob in Saudi Arabia. He stops buying our jet planes and British Aerospace has to hang a "for sale" sign outside its front door.'

'We can't pull anybody?' asked Dempsey. 'Look but don't touch.'

'Not unless you've got something better than drunk and disorderly. I can do without 'em screaming harassment at this unit, all right? That's official!'

'Yeah, but what's *un*official, sir?' asked Dempsey knowingly.

Spikings eyed him for a few seconds then said softly, 'Play it any way you can find, as long as I don't get to hear about it.' He looked down at the file. 'This Ferris character, the manager, a friend of yours, is he?'

'We get along.'

'Start with him. Find out how the place ticks. This one's too neat not to have somebody on the inside, so find 'em.'

Dempsey nodded.

'What about Bessel?' asked Makepeace. 'Can I pull some strings on him? Quietly?'

'Pull whatever you want. Just don't say "police" while you're doing it.' He closed the file and stared challengingly at them. 'Well, don't just sit there. Get moving!'

As they stood up he added testily, 'And, Dempsey, for God's sake go and change out of that costume. You look like Dracula after a heavy night in the blood bank.'

The early morning air was crisp and clear. The breath from the joggers puffing their way around Hyde Park glistened mistily in the bright morning light and the overnight dew was still thick on the grass.

Makepeace was leaning with her back against a tree watching two male joggers approach. The one in the lead was about twenty years old with the physique, blond hair and tan of a Malibu beach boy. The jogger behind him was very different. He was in his early forties, overweight and with an alarmingly florid complexion. He was gazing at the runner ahead of him with a look of blatant adoration in his eyes.

Makepeace waited for the youth to go by then stepped out from under the tree. 'Hallo, Roger! In training for your first heart attack?'

The florid-faced man reacted with surprise. 'Harry, my darling!' he gasped as he came to a halt. 'What on earth are you doing here at this time of the morning?'

'Looking for you, darling. I want to talk to you,' Makepeace told him.

He looked regretfully at the departing back of the blond youth. 'Harry dear, you do ask a *lot* of me, you know . . .'

'He's much too young for you, Roger, you cradle-snatcher.'

'There's no such thing as *too* young, darling. And I've put a lot of work into him . . . It's taken me a week of training just to reach the point where I can keep up with him.'

'I'm doing you a favour,' said Makepeace. 'You'd have dropped dead before you even made a pass at him. Come on, I'll buy you breakfast. Your choice of venue.'

He brightened. 'It's a deal, Harry. I'm absolutely starving.' He gave the youth one last glance. 'There's always plenty more hunks in the park . . .'

He chose Dominique's, one of the most expensive and fashionable pâtisseries in Knightsbridge. Makepeace counted three famous American film stars and two prominent politicians while she waited for Roger Watts to devour an enormous amount of French pastry.

Finally, when he'd finished off the last croissant and was sipping his coffee, into which he'd poured a large brandy, he sighed and said, 'All right, Harry darling. What can Fleet Street's Prince of Darkness do for you?'

'I want to talk about James Bessel.'

22

'You do? How fascinating!' He grinned happily. 'Don't tell me the little shit is in trouble with the cops!'

'No, he's not in any trouble,' said Makepeace quickly. 'This is strictly unofficial.'

His face fell. 'What a pity.'

'I gather you don't like him.'

He grimaced. 'No, I don't. He threatened to sue me for libel once. For something I wrote about him in my column.'

'I don't blame him. I'm tempted to do the same whenever you write about me.'

'But the item was *true*, darling. That's what so irked me. He got the American ambassador's daughter into trouble and then just walked away from the situation, denying everything. There was a frightful ruckus behind the scenes. I merely hinted at what had happened and the writs fell like confetti . . .'

'So the Honourable Jamie is something of a womanizer?' asked Makepeace.

'Womanizer? My dear, he's the Roger Watts of heterosexuals.'

'Goodness, he *must* be a sexual prodigy,' said Makepeace dryly.

'I kid you not, darling. He's been in the pants of every deb in town . . . at least twice.'

'What else is he known for apart from his love life?'

Watts took another sip of coffee. 'Gambling. He's a permanent fixture in all the casinos. Next to laying Sloane Rangers, gambling is his favourite occupation.'

'Is he a winner or a loser?'

'The latter, I'd say, darling. Recently anyway. Dropped a bundle at Asper's last week, I heard. Twenty-four grand in one night.'

'Hmmm,' said Makepeace thoughtfully. 'But I suppose his family is good for any losses. They *are* one of the richest in the country.'

'If not *the* richest, apart from the Windsors and the Vesteys,' agreed Watts. Then he lowered his voice and

23

said, 'But I have heard rumours that the golden teat might have been turned off in Master Bessel's case.'

'Really?' asked Makepeace, sitting upright in her chair.

'It *is* only a rumour,' cautioned Watts. 'And from not a particularly reliable source.'

'That's never stopped you printing rumours before.'

Watts laughed. 'True, darling, but Master Jamie is off-limits to me these days. Proprietor's orders and all that. He wasn't very happy about the legal altercation last time. Turned out he was a close friend of the Bessel family . . .'

Makepeace frowned. 'How can I find out if the rumour is true? Who would know?'

'Harry, darling, I'm not saying another word until you tell me what this is all about. Why are the police suddenly so interested in little Jimmy?'

'Who said this has anything to do with the police?' asked Makepeace warily. 'I told you it was unofficial. Perhaps I'm just interested in joining his long line of conquests.'

Watts looked scornful. '*You*, darling? Pull the other one – it's covered in baby oil. Now tell me the truth. What has the little shit been up to?'

'I'm sorry, Roger. I can't tell you anything. At the moment there are just some vague suspicions about him, that's all.'

'Well, I suppose that's better than nothing.'

'Look, you can't breathe a word of this to anyone,' warned Makepeace. 'And I don't want to see it surfacing in your column.'

'So what's in it for me?' asked Watts bluntly.

Makepeace considered this, then said, 'If anything does break I'll see that you're among the first to get the full story. All right?'

He nodded. 'It's a deal.'

'Now tell me – who would know about Bessel's financial situation?'

24

'Your best bet, darling, is to ask an old schoolfriend of yours.'

'What?'

Watts gave a smug smile. 'I kid you not. Her name is Annabel Smythe-Graves. You were both at school together, I know.'

Makepeace regarded him with genuine astonishment. 'Is there anything you don't know, Roger?'

He shrugged. 'It's my bread and butter, knowing everything there is to know about you upper classes.'

'So why would Annabel be able to tell me about Bessel?'

'She was the nearest thing to a regular bedmate he's had. In between the Sloane Rangers he would always return to poor Annabel. Now, however, he's apparently hanging his socks elsewhere.'

'And I suppose you could tell me where I can locate Annabel as well?'

'You *are* out of touch, dear. Annabel runs a trendy little bookshop in Chelsea. Bought by Daddy, of course.'

'Roger, you're a marvel.'

'I know,' he agreed seriously. Then he pointed at the untouched croissant on her plate. 'Do you mind, darling?'

She handed it over.

Roz Carpenter was still in the same black dress she'd been wearing when dealing the cards at Prince Razul's blackjack table. She had no coat and the fresh morning air had raised goose-bumps on her bare arms and shoulders but she was oblivious to the cold as she hurried down the small and fashionable cobbled mews in Holland Park.

At the end of the mews she pressed a doorbell and waited impatiently. She was just about to ring the bell again when the door was opened.

James Bessel stood there, a half-empty glass of champagne in his hand. He stared at her with bleary, red-rimmed eyes.

'This is pretty stupid of you,' he told her angrily, looking past her up the deserted mews. 'What are you doing here?'

'Murder was pretty stupid too. That's what I'm here for. I want to talk to you about it.'

CHAPTER FOUR

Peter Ferris stood in the gallery above the tiled splendour of the Porchester Baths swimming pool. He was watching a group of five little girls among the other early-morning swimmers. Every so often one of the girls – a pretty eight-year-old – would look up at him and wave, and he would return the wave, forcing himself to smile.

Dempsey hesitated before approaching Ferris. For about half a minute he remained by the door to the gallery and watched the casino manager. Ferris looked older and more haggard than he had the night before – he was obviously a man with a lot of worries.

'Hi, Peter,' said Dempsey as he joined him at the balcony.

Ferris turned and looked at him with surprise. 'Mr Dempsey . . . or should I say *Detective* Dempsey . . . ?'

'James will do fine. Look, I'm sorry I lied about being a cop but, well, you know how it is . . . People get nervous round cops.'

'I wonder why,' said Ferris dryly. He returned his attention to the little girls in the pool. 'How did you know I was here?'

'Your secretary told me. Said you bring your daughter here on her way to school.'

He nodded. 'It's about the only time I ever get to see her, casino hours being what they are.'

Dempsey looked down at the group of girls. 'Which one is she?'

'The one showing off,' said Ferris with a smile. 'She's like her mother. Needs a constant audience.'

Just then Dempsey saw one of the girls wave at

27

Ferris. She was very pretty with large eyes, coal black hair and olive skin. 'That her?'

'Yeah. Name's Julie.'

'She's going to be really something when she gets older. She's a looker . . .'

'Don't I know it,' said Ferris regretfully. 'I dread her approaching adolescence. If there was a drug you could buy that would postpone puberty I'd pay a fortune for it . . . I forsee nothing but boy-trouble . . .' He shook his head. 'You got any kids?'

'Nope. I sometimes wish I had though.'

Ferris turned and looked at him. 'I still don't understand how you – an American – can be working in the British police force.'

'It's a long story. Too long. I'll tell you about it someday if you like but right now there are other things we've got to talk about.'

He gave a resigned nod. 'Yeah. I know. Have you people figured out how they got the money away yet?'

'The forensic boys are still working on it,' said Dempsey. 'But one thing seems pretty certain. It was an inside job.'

'I was afraid that was the conclusion that would be reached.' He sighed. 'Am I on the list of suspects?'

'Yeah, I guess you are,' admitted Dempsey. 'Not high up, though, if that's any consolation.'

'Not much of one. And it won't be just the police who'll have me on their list. The casino owners will be thinking similar thoughts about me. At the very least they'll blame me for not checking out my staff better.'

'And just how well *do* you check out your staff?' Dempsey asked bluntly.

'Pretty thoroughly. We make sure they don't have a criminal record and we demand good references. I personally call all their previous employers to make sure the facts tally and to get first-hand impressions of the applicants concerned . . .'

'What about your dealers – those girls. You know if any of them has associations with a known criminal?'

'Now you're asking a lot. I don't keep tabs on their private lives.'

'But they're not allowed to get involved with the members, are they?'

'That's true. It's a house rule,' said Ferris.

'So how do you make sure they don't break the rule?'

'Well, the pit bosses keep an eye out for that sort of thing. Any giveaway sign between a girl and a member. And the girls themselves know they'd be risking a hell of a lot if they were found to be involved with a member. They wouldn't just lose their job at our casino, they'd lose their dealers' licence too.'

Dempsey considered this for a few moments then asked, 'What about your members – you keep a check on them as well?'

Ferris nodded. 'Oh yes, we get to know their gambling habits and their financial and social backgrounds. Anything that would have a bearing on their relationship with the casino. It's tighter than it might look to the casual visitor . . .'

'Tell your security guy that,' said Dempsey, more harshly than he meant to.

Ferris swallowed. A shade guiltily he said, 'Yeah. Poor Greg. He was only twenty-six. Planned to get married in October. I had to call his girl this morning and tell her . . .' His voice trailed away.

'How soon do you get to hear when one of your members becomes a credit risk?'

'Fairly fast. The grapevine is efficient in these matters.' He looked curiously at Dempsey. 'Why? You think a customer could be behind the robbery?'

'It's a possibility. Are any of them in financial trouble at the moment?'

Ferris shook his head. 'None that I know of.'

'What about that guy who caused the ruckus last night?'

'Bessel? He's filthy with money.'

'Has he lost a lot recently at your place?'

'No more than usual. Why?'

'I was thinking it might be a case of sour grapes. Maybe him or one of your other members resents dropping a bundle at your tables and simply decided to take it back.'

'I suppose so,' said Ferris doubtfully.

'That Arab, for example. He looked the kind of guy who is used to taking just whatever he wants.'

'Prince Razul? No, out of the question. Besides, he's been *winning* recently.'

Dempsey frowned. 'Even so, there's something about him that's been nagging at me – something that had happened last night that I can't put my finger on.'

'No,' said Ferris firmly, 'I just can't believe Prince Razul could be involved. Why would a man of his wealth and position want to rob a casino?'

'That's the four hundred thousand pound question,' said Dempsey.

James Bessel was sprawled across his sofa and watching Roz Carpenter as she paced up and down the living room. He had a calm smile on his face but his eyes revealed his irritation.

'Stop acting so jumpy, Roz,' he drawled. 'Sit down, relax and have a drink. You should be celebrating . . .'

'*Celebrating*?!' She stopped her pacing and turned to him. 'Celebrating what? That I could be arrested as an accessory to murder? Why didn't you tell me you and your friend planned to kill Greg?'

'Would you have agreed to cooperate if you'd known?' he asked.

'No, of course not!'

'I wonder.'

'What's *that* supposed to mean?' she demanded.

'That you must have known someone was going to get hurt last night. Surely you didn't think we were going to walk away with nearly a half a million pounds without *some* blood being spilt. So you left the dirty work to us and now you're acting all surprised and innocent . . .'

'No, that's not true!' she cried. 'I had absolutely no idea that there'd be any violence. You never *told* me there would be!'

'The fact of the matter is, Roz darling, that you're in as deeply as we are and all your protestations of innocence won't change that. You were perfectly willing to take a share of the money – and all the other things . . .' He gestured at the cameo necklace she was wearing. '. . . so now you have to share in the risks.'

'I am *not* going to sit still and be arrested for a murder I had nothing to do with!'

'Roz,' he said calmly, 'Nobody is going to be arrested for murder. The job went perfectly. The police have nothing to go on. We're all absolutely safe. You have nothing to worry about.'

'I'd better not, Jamie. Or else.'

His eyes narrowed. 'What's that supposed to mean?' he asked softly.

'What it sounded like,' she replied, lifting her chin defiantly. 'At the first sign of the police getting anywhere near the truth I'm going to tell them everything. About you, and your partner . . .'

Bessel just stared at her for several long moments in silence, then finally he said, sadly, 'You've really disappointed me, Roz. What happened to all those passionate declarations you made to me? How you'd do anything for me – anything at all?'

'I meant it . . . then.'

'What's changed?'

'You have. The man I said those things to wasn't a murderer.'

'I didn't shoot Greg.'

'You didn't pull the trigger but you're just as guilty.'

Bessel's eyes had lost their alcoholic bleariness – he was completely sober now as he studied her face. Then he smiled at her and stood up. 'I still feel the same about you, Roz,' he said gently.

She took a step backwards. 'No, don't touch me . . . that won't do any good . . .'

He ignored her command and embraced her. She tried to struggle out of his arms. 'No . . .!' she cried. 'Don't!'

He kissed her hard on the mouth. Her struggling ceased and her body went limp in his arms. When the kiss ended and he began to caress the side of her neck with the tip of his tongue she leaned her head back and groaned, 'Damn you . . . damn you . . .'

Bessel then slipped the thin straps down over her shoulders and slowly eased the black evening dress downwards, freeing her breasts. She shivered and dug her fingers into his back as he bent forward and began to gently tongue her left nipple.

She didn't resist when he led her to the sofa, laid her down on it and quickly removed the rest of her clothing.

'Dempsey, would you mind repeating that last statement? I think there's something wrong with the radio.'

'I said, Chief, that I'm at the Baths. Porchester Baths, to be exact. I'm parked out front of them,' said Dempsey into the mike.

The radio crackled irritably. Then, with exaggerated politeness, Spikings said, 'Why are you at Porchester Baths, Dempsey? Is there something wrong with your own bathroom?'

'Ferris, sir,' explained Dempsey. 'I came here to talk to him.'

'But why at the Baths . . .? Oh, never mind – look

Dempsey, we got the forensic report on the casino . . . seems the money went out of a skylight. A very small skylight that wasn't big enough to be covered by the alarm system. Much too small for a body to get through but big enough to pass the money through.'

Dempsey tapped his fingers thoughtfully on the steering wheel. 'What about the roof? Easy access?'

'Easy if you don't mind climbing a wall or two. Clarges Place is about fifty feet away, at the back. Sweet, eh?'

'So that means it was definitely an inside job. There were at least two of them, possibly three. The one who shot the guard and grabbed the money, the one waiting on the roof and maybe someone else who passed the money out, unless it was the same person as the gunman.'

'I agree, Dempsey. At least one casino employee had to be involved,' said Spikings.

'I think I'd better go to the casino and have a look for myself. And another talk to Ferris about his staff . . .'

'Do that, Dempsey,' said Spikings. 'I'll call Make-peace and tell her to meet you there . . .'

Dempsey climbed out of his car and walked back towards the entrance of the Baths. He was halfway there when he saw Ferris emerge accompanied by the five giggling little girls, now all dressed in school uniforms.

Ferris herded them to a nearby grey Mercedes and opened one of the rear doors for them. Four of the girls got in the back – the fifth, Ferris's daughter, had the seat of privilege in the front.

Ferris was about to get in as well when he noticed Dempsey. He frowned. 'I thought you'd left,' he said.

'Just got a call about fresh evidence the forensic boys uncovered. It proves someone in your casino was involved.'

'I see,' said Ferris slowly. His frown deepened.

'I'd like to go back there and have another look

33

around,' said Dempsey. 'And maybe have a longer discussion about your staff. You heading that way now?'

'As soon as I drop the kids off,' Ferris answered distractedly. 'The school's not far. In Holland Park . . .'

Dempsey glanced down and saw Ferris's daughter staring at him with open curiosity through the car window. He winked at her. She looked away in embarrassment. Her friends in the back erupted into a fresh wave of giggling.

Dempsey smiled and said to Ferris, 'The sooner we get this mess cleared up the better it will be for everyone.'

Ferris looked at his daughter and nodded. 'I know,' he said grimly.

Roz lay naked across the sofa in a deep sleep. Bessel, wearing a white bath robe, stood there eyeing her speculatively for a time then went out into the kitchen and picked up a phone.

'Steve? It's me. Listen, this is bad . . . the bloody girl's freaked out. The first sign of the cops sniffing at her heels and she's going to drop us both in it up to our necks. I've got her calmed down now but I don't think we can trust her. She's going to panic, I know it . . .' He paused, listening to the voice on the other end, then said defensively, 'Yes, I *know* she was my choice but she seemed the right one at the time . . .' He paused again. Then, 'What do I want you to do? Well, I want you to *fix* her, of course. As soon as possible.'

CHAPTER FIVE

The casino seemed a different place to Dempsey as he walked through the lobby with Ferris. Its night-time atmosphere of glamour and electric tension was completely absent in the daylight. The air was heavy with stale cigarette smoke and despite the expensive furnishings the place appeared almost seedy.

Dempsey followed Ferris upstairs and into a small reception area. An attractive woman in her early thirties sat behind a desk next to a door marked 'Manager'. She looked agitated.

'Peter, you've got visitors,' she said in a low, urgent voice. 'Mr Prentiss. And he's not alone. That American who's been here before – Ottiano – is with him. And someone else they didn't introduce. Looks like a minder. Should I get Nick up here?' Her hand hovered over a phone.

'No, it's okay, Diana. Everything will be fine.' He gave her a strained smile then looked at Dempsey. 'Perhaps you'd better wait out here, James. A business meeting, I'm afraid.'

'Who are these guys?' asked Dempsey.

'Prentiss heads the consortium that owns the casino. Ottiano is, let's say, a "silent partner".'

Dempsey said, 'If you don't mind, I'd like to sit in on your meeting. But don't tell them I'm a cop. Pass me off as an old friend.' Dempsey grinned. '. . . In the oil business.'

Ferris looked doubtful but nodded and opened the door to his office.

Only one of the three men in the office smiled at them as Ferris and Dempsey entered. He was a tall, fair-haired man in his early fifties with the physical

35

bearing of an ex-soldier. 'Peter!' he cried as he got up from the chair he'd been sitting in. 'Lovely to see you again, old man. Even though the circumstances are a bit rum.' He spoke like the Duke of Edinburgh.

The other two men were so different from the first they could have belonged to a separate species. Both had barrel chests, swarthy skins and heavy five o'clock shadows even though it was not much after 9 am. One of them was leaning over Ferris's desk, reading through the papers on it, while the other was sprawled out in a leather armchair. Their expressions were cold and suspicious.

'Hi, Ferris,' said the one at the desk. 'Who's he?' He pointed a thumb at Dempsey. He had an American accent.

'An old friend, Mr Ottiano. Name's James Dempsey,' said Ferris. 'James – Mr Ottiano. And Mr Prentiss . . .'

The tall Englishman shook Dempsey's hand and said jovially, 'Delighted to meet you, old chap . . .'

Ottiano, however, simply scowled and said, 'Beat it, Mr Dempsey. We got some important business to discuss with your friend here – in private.'

'I'd prefer to stay, if you don't mind,' said Dempsey.

A flicker of surprise appeared in Ottiano's eyes when he heard Dempsey's accent. Then he growled, 'Yeah, I *do* mind. Beat it, I said.'

Dempsey didn't move.

Ottiano turned to the other Italian who so far hadn't said a word. 'Cal, help this guy out of here.'

Cal lumbered to his feet and began to advance on Dempsey. Dempsey was surprised that his knuckles didn't quite brush the floor as he walked.

Prentiss, a pained expression on his face, stepped between Dempsey and the advancing Cal. 'I say, I really don't think this sort of thing is at all necessary,' he told Ottiano. 'If Peter's friend wants to stay I see no reason why he shouldn't.' He turned and gave

Ferris an appealing look. 'Your friend will treat anything he hears in the strictest confidence, won't he Peter?'

'Certainly,' said Ferris, without enthusiasm.

Cal halted and looked to Ottiano for guidance. Ottiano frowned at Prentiss then at Dempsey. Finally he nodded. 'Okay, he can stay. Providing he keeps his damned mouth shut.'

Cal returned to his chair, a suggestion of disappointment on his face.

Ottiano came out from behind the desk and approached Ferris. 'Well, let's hear it. And it better be good.'

'Hear what?' asked Ferris in a calm, level voice.

'Your explanation on how someone can lift four hundred grand out of this casino without anyone seeing a goddamn thing!'

Ferris spread his hands helplessly. 'Mr Ottiano, I just don't know. The police think it was an inside job . . .'

'Hey, what a coincidence,' said Ottiano with heavy sarcasm. 'We came to the same conclusion. Now what we want to know is *who* pulled it off.'

'I don't know,' said Ferris, shaking his head. 'It's a complete mystery. I've wracked my brains trying to figure out a likely candidate but so far no luck . . .'

'Well, that's too bad, Ferris, 'cause as far as we're concerned you're carrying the can for this missing four hundred grand. You're the one responsible for keeping tabs on your staff so that makes you responsible for what they get up to, right?'

'What do you expect me to do?' Ferris asked him. 'If the police haven't got a lead yet how am I supposed to find out who stole the money?'

Ottiano grinned at him, displaying nicotine-stained teeth. 'That's your problem, Ferris. Let me just say that unless you get results you're in big trouble. And I mean *big* trouble. Know what I mean?'

Ferris looked at Prentiss. 'Is that official?'

Prentiss refused to look him in the eye. Flushing with embarrassment he muttered, 'Sorry, old boy, but I'm afraid it's out of my hands.'

'Jesus Christ,' Ferris said disgustedly. 'I've flogged myself to death for the casino, often working twenty-four hours at a stretch, and this is how I'm treated at the first sign of trouble.'

'Turn off the bleeding heart, Ferris,' sneered Ottiano. 'Losing nearly half a million pounds ain't just trouble, it's a fucking catastrophe. And how do we know you didn't lift it yourself?'

Ferris reddened. 'You make an accusation like that about me and I expect you to back it up with some evidence, otherwise take it back.'

'I'm not taking nothing back,' said Ottiano. 'What I'm telling you is that you've got a week to find that four hundred grand. If you know where it is your job is easy; if you don't then you'd better get your ass into gear and start looking. Savvy?'

Dempsey said, 'Forgive me for butting in, but I think you're being kind of hard on Peter here. He's a victim of whoever pulled off the robbery just as much as you are.'

Ottiano turned and glared at him. 'No, I don't forgive you for butting in. I told you to keep your mouth shut so *keep* it shut!'

Dempsey smiled and said softly, 'Sorry, no can do. You see, I'm sort of involved in all this and my advice to you is to lay off Peter. Or else.'

'Oh yeah?' sneered Ottiano. 'Cal, get this bum outta here. He had his chance . . .'

Cal heaved himself out of his chair again and moved in on Dempsey. Dempsey drew the Magnum out of his shoulder holster with fluid speed, stepped forward and slammed the barrel against the side of Cal's head, just above his right ear.

Cal blinked, grunted and then sagged down onto

one knee in front of Dempsey. Dempsey shoved the end of the barrel into Cal's mouth, chipping a front tooth as he did so.

'Mr Ottiano, unless you order this gorilla of yours to back off you're going to have to buy him a new brain.'

There was a stunned silence in the room for at least fifteen seconds. Ottiano stared at Dempsey in blank-eyed surprise; Ferris and Prentiss both looked as if they desperately wanted to be somewhere else, and Cal just looked terrified.

Finally Ottiano glanced disgustedly at Ferris and said, 'So you hired yourself some muscle, did you? Well, it won't do you any good . . .'

'I'm not "muscle", Ottiano, I'm a cop,' said Demp-sey harshly. 'And *you're* the one in trouble. You see, I know you, pal. You're a member of the Colombo family, one of the five big Mafia families that run New York City. The last I heard of you you were in Atlantic City. What happened – you get a transfer?'

Ottiano's lower jaw dropped. 'You're a *cop!*' he cried. Then, 'Hey, what's the charge? I'm telling you, man, you'll have a hell of a time trying to extradite me – my lawyers will wrap you in so much red tape you'll be here till the next century!'

Dempsey couldn't help smiling. Ottiano had pre-sumed that he, being an American, had been sent to take him back to the States. 'Relax,' he said. 'I'm not trying to nail you. I'm only interested in finding out who robbed your casino and murdered your guard.' He turned to Prentiss. 'But I'm sure the British Gam-ing Board would be interested to know that your consortium, Mr Prentiss, has connections with some-one like Mr Ottiano here . . .'

'Are you really a police officer?' asked Prentiss in a dazed voice. He had suddenly broken out in a sweat. He pulled an immaculately pressed white handkerchief from his jacket's top pocket and began to dab at his face.

Dempsey nodded. He withdrew the barrel of the .44 from Cal's mouth and, with his other hand, produced his S.I.10 identification. Prentiss read it and blanched. 'Oh dear,' he said.

'I still don't geddit,' rasped Ottiano. 'What's an American doing working with the Brit police . . .?'

'*Shut up!*' snapped Prentiss unexpectedly. 'You've said more than enough this morning. From now on leave the talking to me!' He turned to Dempsey and gave a forced smile. 'I'm sure, Mr Dempsey, that this misunderstanding can be sorted out . . .'

'Sure it can,' said Dempsey equably. 'You take the pressure off my friend Peter here and you leave the job of finding the guys who hit your casino to the police. I hear one little hint of a threat against him and I make a call to the Gaming Board. Get me?'

'Yes. The message is quite clear, Mr Dempsey,' said Prentiss, dabbing more frantically at his forehead.

'Good. Now take your trash and go,' said Dempsey, gesturing with the .44.

Ottiano scowled and opened his mouth to protest but Prentiss cut him short. 'You heard the gentleman. I really do think it would be in our best *interests* to do as he says. Do you follow?'

After a pause Ottiano reluctantly nodded. He came and helped Cal to his feet, glaring at Dempsey as he did so.

As the three of them were going out the door Dempsey said, 'Mr Prentiss, one more thing.'

Prentiss stopped and turned, his expression wary. 'Yes?'

'In view of the long hours Peter has been putting into your casino I think he deserves a rise. Don't you?'

Prentiss nodded. 'Yes, I do. I'll see to it immediately.' He closed the door.

40

In the silence that followed Ferris let out a long sigh. Then he said, 'Thanks . . .'

'My pleasure,' said Dempsey.

Ferris went to a drinks cabinet in the corner of the room and opened it. 'I don't normally indulge this early in the day but right now I could do with a drink. A large one. How about you?'

'Sure. Scotch on the rocks.'

As Ferris handed him his drink Dempsey frowned. 'You know, that creep Ottiano may have done us a favour.'

'What do you mean?'

'When he mistook me for a hired bodyguard – it jogged my memory about something that's been nagging at me. Something that happened last night – before the guard got shot.'

'What was it?' asked Ferris curiously.

'The guy Prince Razul came with – a minder, right?'

'Yes. Name's Crane. He's never far away from the Prince when he's gambling . . .'

'So where was he when Bessel started acting up?' asked Dempsey. 'I remember the Prince just missed getting kicked by him but I don't remember his bodyguard moving in. In fact I don't remember seeing his bodyguard around at all during the struggle with Bessel. Do you?'

Ferris frowned thoughtfully. Then he said, 'In all the excitement I can't say positively he wasn't there – I was too busy – but I don't remember seeing Crane again until later.'

'Did the uniform guys take a statement from him last night?'

'I'm not sure. I know they talked to Razul before he left . . . Crane might have been getting the car . . .'

'I'll check it out. And Crane too.'

'You think that Crane was involved?'

Dempsey shrugged. 'He sure had the opportunity. And being a security guy himself he could probably go anywhere around here without arousing the suspicion of your security people. It's like the Romans used to say, *quid custodiat* something or other . . .'

'Meaning what?'

'Means you can have bodyguards, but who's keeping an eye on *them*?'

CHAPTER SIX

As Dempsey was walking out through the casino lobby he ran into Makepeace who was just coming in the front door.

'So this is where you spend all your free time,' she said, looking around with an expression of disapproval. 'I can't say I'm very impressed.'

'You should see it by night, princess. It's a different world. If you play your cards right I'll invite you along sometime.'

'I'm not a card player, so don't bother. I've better things to do with my spare time.'

'Yeah. Things like chrome-plating your chastity belt, no doubt.'

She bristled. 'I'll ignore that. Have you made any progress on the case this morning or have you just been practising your dice rolls or whatever?'

'Yeah, I think I got a solid lead . . .' He told her about Razul's bodyguard, Crane.

She nodded thoughtfully. 'Sounds promising. My bet is that Crane and Bessel were working together.'

'But why would a rich guy like Bessel want to get mixed up in a robbery?'

'That's what we're going to find out right now,' Makepeace told him. 'From an old schoolfriend of mine.'

Annabel Smythe-Graves' bookshop was located in Culford Gardens, just off Sloane Square. It was a small establishment and, to Dempsey's eye, looked as if it had been built in Shakespeare's time.

He peered in through one of the windows but

couldn't see anyone inside. 'You think this Annabel person is going to pour her heart out to you about Bessel?' he asked Makepeace.

'If she's in the mood, yes. She never did like losing, whether it was at hockey or boyfriends.' Makepeace pushed the door open and entered. Dempsey followed her.

The interior of the shop was cramped. Rows of bookshelves, with very little space between them, formed a kind of rats' maze that led towards the rear of the building.

'Business ain't exactly booming,' observed Dempsey. The shop appeared deserted apart from them.

Then, from around a corner, came a tall, statuesque girl with long black hair. She was dressed in tight, black jeans, boots and a black shirt that was open at least two buttons more than was really necessary to show how well developed she was. Dempsey's spirits immediately rose.

'Good morning,' said the girl with a formal smile. 'Can I help . . .' Her eyes widened with surprise as she recognized Makepeace then she gave a squeal of delight and pushed past Dempsey.

He watched approvingly, and a little enviously, as the two women hugged each other happily.

'Harry!' cried Annabel. 'It's been simply *yonks* since I've seen you! Let me look at you!' She held Makepeace at arms' length and surveyed her critically. 'Good. You've lost weight. Especially around the hips which is where you needed to lose it most of all. Remember all the ragging you used to get in the showers? We used to call you "wobblebum" . . .'

Makepeace cleared her throat and gestured at Dempsey. 'Uh, Ann, I'd like you to meet my colleague, James Dempsey.'

Annabel turned and inspected him. Dempsey felt like he was being scrutinized by a pair of security cameras. She finally gave her verdict. 'Very nice,' she told Makepeace, as she held out her hand for Dempsey to shake.

'Opinions differ,' said Makepeace.

'Pay no attention to her, Annabel. I *am* very nice,' he said, noticing how her hand lingered in his.

'You're American,' she said, surprised. 'When Harry said you were a colleague I presumed you were another cop.'

'I am.'

'He's over here learning how to do police work the right way,' said Makepeace. 'But he's still got a way to go.'

Annabel shook her head in wonder. 'I can't get used to you being a policewoman, Harry,' she told Makepeace. 'Who'd ever thought that little, shy Harriet Makepeace would end up a cop . . .'

'Ol' Wobblebum wasn't likely police material, eh?' asked Dempsey.

'Gosh, no! Her other nickname at school was "Mouse".'

'Uh, how's *your* line of work coming along, Ann?' asked Makepeace hurriedly.

'Can't complain. I deal in both modern first editions and antiquarian books and there's a lot of money to be made in both fields at the moment. With the dollar so strong against the pound there are herds of Yank collectors coming over looking for bargains. I sold the Tolkien *Lord of the Rings* trilogy to a guy from New York yesterday for nine hundred and fifty pounds. The books only cost me four hundred so that's a profit to me of over one hundred per cent.'

'Where do you get your stock from?' asked Dempsey.

'Oh, I have this marvellous little man who scours the country on my behalf. Goes to all the auctions, book fairs and out-of-the-way secondhand shops.'

'Sounds like you're onto a good thing,' said Makepeace.

'I am,' she agreed. 'But I'm sure you and your

handsome friend haven't dropped in to discuss the book trade. What's up?' She looked questioningly at both of them.

'Actually, Ann, we want to talk to you about an ex-boyfriend of yours,' said Makepeace.

Annabel raised her eyebrows. 'An old boyfriend of *mine*? You intrigue me! Who?'

'Jamie Bessel.'

Her expression turned ugly so quickly it was like seeing a sudden jump-cut in a movie. 'That bastard,' she sneered. 'What's he been up to?'

'I take it he and you are no longer on good terms,' said Makepeace.

Annabel gave a harsh laugh. 'That's putting it mildly. The last time I saw him he snatched back a necklace he'd given me. A little cameo on a gold chain. Even worse, I was wearing it at the time. He tore it straight off my neck when I bumped into him in the street. Look – you can still see the mark . . .' She leaned towards Dempsey, bending her neck.

'Terrible. You could have lost your head,' he told her, though he couldn't see a mark on her very white skin.

She looked up at him and smiled.

'And when did that happen?' asked Makepeace, a little frostily.

'Last month. About five weeks ago, I guess.'

'You haven't seen him since?'

'No.' Her face turned ugly again. 'Neither do I want to, thank you. But a friend of mine – Clare – saw him in Kensington last week. He was with some little bitch who Clare didn't recognize. She said she looked rather common but then Jamie always did have a weakness for scrubbers. Though these days they're probably all he can afford . . .'

'Really? I thought he was rolling in money,' said Makepeace.

'He *was*, but . . .' She lowered her voice to a conspiratorial whisper. 'If you want a family secret, his father has cut him off without the proverbial penny.'

'Where'd you get this?' asked Dempsey. 'From him?'

'No. He never said a word about it. I read it in a letter from his father while I was staying at his place one night.' She shrugged. 'I'm an avid reader . . .'

'I can see that,' said Dempsey, looking around the shop.

'You going to tell me what this is about?' asked Annabel. 'I gather Jamie's in trouble.'

'Possibly, yes, he is,' said Makepeace. 'But we can't say anything about it yet.'

'I hope it's big trouble,' said Annabel. And smiled.

Outside in the street Dempsey said, 'Were all the girls at your school like her?'

'Good heavens, no. Annabel was always rather out of the ordinary – a bit wilder than anyone else, the school rebel and so on. Everyone adored her. Especially the younger girls who hero-worshipped her.' Makepeace smiled to herself. 'In fact I had quite a pash on her myself for a time.'

'A *pash*? What the hell is that?'

'Oh, just schoolgirl talk for . . . forget it, Dempsey.'

He grinned at her. 'You mean you and she . . . ?'

'I said, forget it, Dempsey.'

'Don't worry, your secret is safe with me . . . Wobblebum.'

Makepeace narrowed her eyes at him. 'If I ever hear you say that name again I'll shoot you with your own .44.'

He held up his hands in mock surrender. 'Hey, I give you my word, never again. Honest injun.'

She turned on her heel and headed for her car.

'Now what?' he called as he hurried after her. 'Do we go pick up Bessel and squeeze his head a little and see if it fits?'

47

'Fits what? Being broke and snatching back neck-laces? He'd laugh at us and you'd stick that gun of yours up his nose and I'd be on traffic work next week. No thank you.' She opened her car door and got in.

'But Princess, we got a motive for him now. And like you said, it looks as if he and this Crane guy were working together . . .'

'It may *look* like it but we haven't got any solid evidence yet. We've got to find a connection between them. And that involves good old ordinary police work – not head squeezing. So let's go back to headquarters and check the files.' She slammed the door and started the engine.

Dempsey stepped back and watched her Jaguar roar off. Then he rubbed his chin thoughtfully, turned around and walked back to Annabel's bookshop.

Makepeace was at the console of the S.I.10 computer, with Spikings leaning over her shoulder, when Demp-sey walked into the office over an hour later.

'Any luck?' he asked.

They both looked up at him and frowned. 'Did you get caught in a traffic jam or something?' asked Makepeace. 'I got back here ages ago.'

'I went and had another little talk with your old school buddy.'

'Oh yes?' said Makepeace suspiciously. 'And what was the result?'

'We're having dinner tomorrow night.'

'Dempsey, I'd appreciate it if you would kindly make your social arrangements during your *own* time,' growled Spikings.

'Yessir,' said Dempsey.

Makepeace shook her head disgustedly. 'You've bitten off more than even you can chew with Annabel, Dempsey. She'll have you for breakfast.'

'That's what I'm counting on,' he said, with a leer.

'Do you mind if we get back to *work*!' exclaimed Spikings. 'Harry, keep digging. There's got to be something on record that we can use.'

'What have you got on Crane so far?' asked Dempsey.

'Not much,' said Makepeace. 'All we know is that his full name is Stephen Richard Crane, he's thirty-seven years old and he was hired by Prince Razul through a security firm called Protel. I checked up on them and they're very scrupulous about their people. They don't hire anyone with a criminal record but I'm going through the CR files just to make sure. So far no luck...'

'What did Protel have to say about Crane?'

'Only that he's been with them two years and he's good at his work. Their clients have always been satisfied with him.'

'Did Protel check his army record?'

'Yes. It was excellent – honourable discharge and all that. In fact it was one of the main reasons they hired him, but...' Makepeace looked up at Dempsey. 'But how did you know he'd been in the army?'

Dempsey gave a smug grin. 'While I was making my "social arrangements" with your old school friend I asked her if Bessel had any male friends he saw a lot of. She said the only one was a guy he'd been in the army with. The guy had been a sergeant under Bessel in the Guards but Bessel seemed to think very highly of him and was always going out boozing with him. Annabel met him a few times and didn't think much of him – a "real macho-man" in her words...'

'Are you saying what I think you're saying?' asked Spikings.

'Yep. We got our connection. Bessel's old army buddy is Stephen Richard Crane.'

CHAPTER SEVEN

Bessel stood waiting on the corner of Baker Street and Marylebone Road. It was nearly 11.30 and the area was packed with tourists, most of them no doubt heading for the Planetarium or Madame Tussauds. Bessel was holding the same leather bag he'd had the night before.

A burgundy-coloured Rolls-Royce slid to a halt in front of him. He tried to see into it but the windows were tinted and all he could see was his own reflection. Then one of the windows descended with a quiet whine from an electric motor and Bessel saw Crane behind the driver's wheel.

'Hop in,' said Crane.

Bessel opened the door and climbed in. 'What's this, one of the Arab's cast-offs?' he asked as he sank into the upholstery of the front passenger's seat.

'One of them, yeah. The wives use the other.' Crane crossed Marylebone Road and continued on down Baker Street towards Oxford Street. The pre-lunch time traffic was already heavy.

Bessel opened the leather bag. 'Your share's all here. And so's this . . .' He took out the silenced .38 and handed it to Crane butt-first.

Crane took it and casually tossed it into the glove box. 'You did very well – for an officer,' he said.

Bessel grinned. 'Coming from you that's a real compliment. Were you searched?'

'In the lobby. Routine. Has the old bill been sniffing round you yet?'

'No. Not a sign of them. It looks as if it worked perfectly.'

'Except that your little tart's kicking up. I told you she probably would.'

'I know, I know . . . so what are we going to do?'

'Have you given her her share of the lolly yet?'

'No. Told her I'd hang onto it for the time being. In case the police search her place. My bet is they'll check up on all the casino staff.'

Crane nodded. 'You sure she's gonna crack?'

'I don't know, to be honest. I've got her eating out of my hand again but that may be only a temporary situation. Killing Greg has really rattled her.'

'Then we've got no choice. We can't take the chance with her.'

Bessel sighed. 'You're right, but I just wish there was another way. I've become quite fond of her, in spite of everything . . .'

'You're not going soft on me, are you, Captain?'

'Of course not. But . . . well, I don't want anything to do with taking care of her. I'm going to leave it all up to you.'

'Gee, thanks, Captain. You're all heart.'

Dempsey and Makepeace stared expectantly at Spikings who was leaning back in his chair with a deep frown on his face.

'Come on, Chief, just say the word,' pleaded Dempsey. 'Let us loose on Bessel. We got the motive and we got the connection between him and Crane. It all adds up.'

'In theory, yeah,' agreed Spikings doubtfully. 'But it's still all circumstantial evidence. We pick Bessel up on that alone and we'll be knee-deep in lawyers. He might be skint but he's still got access to the family phone numbers. I need something more solid.'

'Then let us go and question Crane,' said Makepeace.

'Yeah, Chief. Give us a body, will you?'

Spikings nodded slowly. 'Okay, you got it. Check him out. If it smells right, pull him in. Then we'll get Bessel.'

'That still leaves the third member of the group,' said Makepeace. 'The one on the casino staff.'

'You sure there is a third member?' asked Spikings.

'Someone had to pass that money out through the skylight to whoever it was on the roof.'

'Well, take care of Crane and Bessel first,' said Spikings. 'You can flush out the third one later. And Dempsey . . .'

'Yessir?'

'No more bodies.'

Dempsey looked pained. 'I never shoot first, sir.'

'Well, try not shooting at all for a change.'

'I'll try, sir, but . . .'

Spikings gave him a dismissive wave of his hand. 'No excuses. You shoot one person on this case, no matter what the provocation, and you'll be back in New York before your gun barrel has time to cool down.'

A knife blade appeared through the gap in the window and pushed aside the old-fashioned swivel-catch. The lower half of the window was slid upwards and Dempsey climbed into the room. As he stood there looking around Makepeace climbed in after him.

'You see? Nothing to it,' he told her cheerfully. 'Funny how crooks are always careless about their own home security arrangements.'

'Hilarious,' she muttered as she brushed dust from her skirt. 'But this is still breaking and entering, Dempsey, and there's a law against it.'

'Listen, the guy's not around – what should we do, stick a message in his letterbox and come back later? "Dear Mister Crane, this is the police; we think you pulled a robbery but since you're not at home we'll try again later . . ." Is that how you English cops handle these situations?'

'We could have waited in the car outside.'

'Yeah, and waste maybe the whole day, if not longer. We got to get our hands on something substantial as soon as possible – so start searching.'

Makepeace surveyed the room with distaste. It was not much more than a large bedsit and Crane was obviously not house-proud. Both tables in the room were littered with dirty dishes and empty food cans; the sheets on the unmade bed were of indeterminate colour and there were stacks of aging newspapers and magazines all over the floor.

She opened the door that led into the tiny bathroom, looked inside and said, 'Yuck!' She shut the door. '*You* can search in there,' she told Dempsey.

Dempsey was rummaging through a cupboard that was full of physical fitness equipment, including a set of barbells. He took out a bullworker and showed it to her. 'The guy may not be clean but he sure likes to keep in shape.'

She went to a chest of drawers and pulled one open. It was full of dirty underwear. 'I am definitely not putting my hand in *there*,' she said firmly.

'Hey, stop fooling around and get to work,' Dempsey told her. 'Stop acting like a woman and start acting like a cop.'

She put her hands on her hips and glared at him. '*You're* certainly not acting like a cop. You're acting like a common housebreaker, and I really shouldn't be aiding and abetting you in this, you know . . .'

'I like you abetting me, Harry. I wish you'd abet me more . . .' He opened another cupboard. This was stacked full of empty Guinness bottles, plus the odd empty bottle of Scotch.

'I know what you'd like,' muttered Makepeace, turning back to the open drawer and pulling it all the way out. She turned it upsidedown and emptied the soiled underwear onto the floor. There was a clunk as a small cardboard box hit the floor as well.

She bent down and picked it up. 'Eureka,' she

murmured. She showed the box to Dempsey. He saw it contained a number of bullets.

'They're .38s,' he said. 'Same make and size as the two they dug out of the security guard.'

'Now who's the real cop around here?' she asked triumphantly.

'You did well, kid. You deserve a great, big kiss.'

She stepped back hurriedly. 'Just try it, buster, and they'll be digging .38s out of *you*.'

Some minutes later, as they were driving through Earl's Court away from Crane's flat, Makepeace got Spikings on the radio and told him what they'd found.

Spikings was pleased. 'I'll put warrants out for Crane's and Bessel's arrest immediately. Now what about number three? Any ideas?'

Makepeace glanced at Dempsey. 'Well?'

He frowned. 'As soon as it gets out that the other two have been picked up the mysterious number three is going to make a run for it. I think we should go to the casino and see who doesn't turn up for work this evening.'

'Sounds reasonable,' said Spikings. 'Go to it. I'll call you when we've got Bessel and his mate under lock and key . . .'

Dempsey grinned at Makepeace. 'This is turning into a piece of cake. Two down and one to go and I haven't had to fire a single shot.'

'If you don't mind I'll wait until tomorrow before I call the Guinness Book of Records,' said Makepeace.

Roz Carpenter opened the door of her flat and stood aside to let Bessel enter. She gave him an uncertain frown as he put the small suitcase down and turned to her. 'I still don't understand why you wanted to come back here,' she said.

'I told you,' he said patiently. 'I don't fancy hanging around my own place for the next couple of days just in case the police do decide I'm worth a visit.' He took hold of her and kissed her gently. 'Besides, it's a lot cosier this way, don't you agree?'

She nodded. 'But I've got to go to work soon . . .'

'Not for another hour, at least. That's plenty of time.' He kissed her again and then led her into the bedroom.

An hour and a half later Bessel was sitting alone with a large whisky in his hand. The TV set was on but he wasn't really watching it. The soft tap at the door made him start when it came, even though he was expecting it.

He got up and opened the door. Crane quickly slipped inside. He was wearing dark glasses and a cap.

Bessel's greeting was lukewarm. 'You've got a long wait,' he told Crane in a subdued voice.

'I don't mind,' said Crane as he took off his cap, glasses and overcoat. 'I'm a very patient character, as you know.' He then took out the silenced .38 revolver and laid it on the table beside the door.

CHAPTER EIGHT

Dempsey slammed the phone down and swore under his breath. 'I don't get it! What's the matter with the cops in this crazy town? They *still* haven't found Bessel *or* Crane.'

Makepeace, who was sitting in one of the armchairs in Peter Ferris's office, said, 'Maybe they got wind of what was happening and made a run for it.'

'Maybe, but so far no one's spotted them at any of the airports, railway stations or ferry terminals.' Dempsey ran a hand through his hair with annoyance. 'It's so goddamned frustrating. I thought we had it all sewn up.'

The door opened and Ferris came in. They both looked at him enquiringly. He shook his head. 'Everyone has turned up for work. A few latecomers as usual, but they're all here and acting normally.'

'Shit,' said Dempsey, with feeling.

'I wish I could help you further,' said Ferris, 'But I still can't imagine which of my people would have been involved with the robbery and Greg's murder . . . I just can't believe it of any of them.'

Makepeace said thoughtfully, 'What if we spread a false rumour that Bessel has already been arrested? That should get a reaction.'

'Yeah. But apart from nailing the third member of Bessel's little gang we've still got to find him and Crane. It's likely that the third guy knows where the other two are staying and can lead us straight to them. But if they think that Bessel's been arrested they'll high-tail it in the opposite direction . . .'

Makepeace nodded. 'I guess you're right. So what are we going to do?'

'I'm working on it. Don't rush me.'

'I still find it hard to believe that Jamie Bessel and Prince Razul's man are behind it all,' said Ferris. 'It all seems so incredible.'

'Well, all the evidence sure points that way,' Dempsey told him. 'And the lab has confirmed that the bullets we found in Crane's flat were identical to the ones that killed your man.'

Ferris sighed. 'I know this business is supposed to turn one into a total cynic but it seems I still have a capacity for being shocked.'

'I'm gonna shock you some more,' said Dempsey. 'Did you ever have any social contact with either Bessel or Crane. Out of working hours, I mean?'

Ferris looked at him and smiled wearily. 'I'm still under suspicion too?'

'*Everyone* here is under suspicion and I'm afraid that includes you, Peter. So what's your answer?'

'You expect me to tell you the truth if I *was* associated with them?'

'No,' admitted Dempsey, 'But we'll find out the truth sooner or later so you could save us a lot of trouble.'

'The truth is I had nothing to do with either of them outside of the casino,' said Ferris. 'Do you believe me?'

'I sure want to,' said Dempsey.

Ferris said, 'Well, I suppose I can't expect a better answer. You have a job to do.' He went to the drinks cabinet and poured himself a large scotch. 'Want one?' he asked Dempsey.

'Yeah, thanks.'

'You're on duty,' said Makepeace disapprovingly.

Dempsey looked at her but said nothing. He took the offered drink from Ferris.

Makepeace shook her head when Ferris asked her if she wanted a drink as well. 'What I want is to *do* something instead of just sitting here twiddling my thumbs.' She stood up and started to pace restlessly around the office.

'Why don't you go for a wander downstairs,' suggested Dempsey. 'After last night the staff know I'm a cop but they don't know you're one. Am I right, Peter?'

'Yes,' said Ferris. 'Only my secretary and Nick know that the Sergeant is a policewoman.'

Makepeace brightened. 'Good idea, Dempsey. I'll do it.'

'I'll call Nick and tell him you're coming down,' said Ferris, picking up the phone.

'While you're down there you can play some blackjack,' Dempsey told her.

'I never gamble,' said Makepeace frostily.

Makepeace's hope of remaining inconspicuous was quickly dashed. She had been in the casino less than thirty seconds when she was approached by a sleek-looking Greek in his mid-forties and propositioned. Apart from feeling resentful at his presumption that she was a call-girl she was also surprised at the amount he was offering for her services. It nearly equalled a month of her police salary.

After politely turning down his offer she escaped towards the blackjack tables. She spent a couple of minutes watching the play at one of the tables, more interested in the smooth skill of the female dealer than in the game itself, before moving on to the adjacent table.

Again her interest was fixed on the woman croupier, admiring the attractive girl's cool effectiveness behind the table. Makepeace was just musing on the implicit eroticism in the dealers' roles – with their air hostess-like briskness combined with their plunging necklines – when she noticed the necklace the girl was wearing. A small, expensive-looking cameo on a gold chain . . .

There was a tap on Makepeace's shoulder. She turned, expecting to be propositioned again, but found herself facing a man she recognized. He was in his late twenties with the distinctive, inbred features of a member of the British aristocracy; the high forehead with the receding hairline of wavy hair and matching receding chin. She couldn't remember his name but knew she'd taken part with him in a clay pigeon shooting competition the month before.

'Harry Makepeace!' he cried in a loud 'Hooray Henry' voice, 'What are *you* doing in this den of vice?'

She gave him a strained smile. 'Oh, hello . . . er . . .'

'It's Graham Locke. Runner up to you in the Bisley shoot, remember?'

To Makepeace it seemed as if his braying voice was carrying right across the casino. 'Yes, of course I remember,' she said uneasily. 'How are you?'

'Better with a small-bore than I am at this game, unfortunately. What about you? I didn't know police-women went in for this sort of thing . . .'

She winced inwardly and glanced at the croupier, but the girl gave no sign of having heard. 'I'm just a guest at the moment, Graham,' Makepeace told Locke. Then, looking at her watch, she said, 'I'm sorry but you'll have to excuse me. I've got to make a call . . .'

She hurried away from him, went out into the lobby then headed upstairs to Ferris's office.

'You were quick,' said Dempsey as she entered. 'Lose your shirt already?'

'You remember Annabel's story about the necklace Bessel snatched back from her?' asked Makepeace urgently.

'How could I forget anything about Annabel?'

'Well, one of the dealers down there is wearing something that could be the very same necklace. Either that or it's a hell of a coincidence.'

'Which dealer?' asked Ferris.

'She's on one of the blackjack tables. The one next to the big pillar . . .'

'That would be Rosalind Carpenter,' said Ferris with a frown. 'She's been with us over a year. Lovely girl, and a good croupier too. Are you *sure* about this necklace, Sergeant? I mean just because it seems similar doesn't mean that Bessel gave it to her. She could have bought herself one, couldn't she?'

'Yes,' agreed Makepeace. 'And if that's the case I'll apologize. But it's a long coincidence . . .'

Dempsey said, 'Would you get her up here, Peter? Right away.'

Ferris sighed. 'I'll get Nick to bring her up, but I can't help feeling you're making a mistake.' He picked up the phone and asked for the pit boss. When Nick Colino came to the phone Ferris said, 'Nick, would you go and ask Roz Carpenter to come and see me in the office right away. Get Mike to fill in at her table while she's away.'

Dempsey and Makepeace waited impatiently for the girl to arrive. When the knock at the door finally came they looked expectantly towards it.

'Come in, Roz,' called Ferris.

The door opened but it wasn't Roz, it was Nick, the pit boss. He looked uncomfortable. 'Couldn't find her, Mr Ferris. She's not at her table or anywhere else. It seems she's gone, sir.'

Ferris was at a loss. 'But . . . I don't understand.' He stared at Makepeace. 'How could she have known?'

'Damn,' muttered Makepeace. 'I bumped into a small bore at her table who knew me. I didn't think she heard him but she must have.'

'Well, let's get after her,' said Dempsey. 'She can't have got far.'

'Wait,' said Makepeace, 'Let's figure out where she might be heading first.' She turned to Nick. 'Did she change into different clothes before she left?'

He shook his head.

'That means she'll probably go home to get into less conspicuous clothes before she makes a run for it. Where does she live?'

'In Maida Vale . . .' said Ferris, hurrying to a filing

cabinet. He got a file out and read, 'Flat 5, Huntley House in Abercorn Place.'

'It's on a corner at the top of the hill just before you get to Abbey Road,' said Nick. 'I've given her a lift home several times.'

'Let's go,' said Dempsey, heading for the door. 'With any luck we might find Bessel there as well . . .'

Stephen Crane sat alone in the darkness in Roz Carpenter's living room. He was facing the front door, a cigarette in his hand and the silenced .38 on his lap.

CHAPTER NINE

James Bessel, sitting in his car on the opposite side of the road from Roz's block of flats, was surprised when the black cab pulled up and Roz got out. He looked at his watch with a frown. What was she doing back so early? What had happened?

He watched her pay off the taxi driver and hurry towards the entrance of her building. He tried not to think of what he knew was waiting for her in her flat upstairs. She looked small and vulnerable as she disappeared inside and he felt a sudden rush of regret for what was about to happen . . .

He remembered their lovemaking that afternoon – the look on her face afterwards – and his hands clenched on the steering wheel . . .

'Put your pedal to the metal!' ordered Dempsey as Makepeace's Jaguar sped up the Edgware Road towards Maida Vale.

'What the hell do you think I'm doing!' she snapped back, swerving to avoid a taxi coming out of a side street. She gave him a blast of her horn and waved her fist at the startled driver.

'You call this fast?' said Dempsey. 'I've seen a dead tortoise move quicker.'

'If you don't shut up I'll put you out at the next corner and you can run along behind!'

Roz Carpenter hurried up the stairs. Her flat was on the third floor and she was panting by the time she reached her landing. The terrible feeling of panic she'd experienced when she'd heard that the blonde girl by her table was a policewoman was still with her as she quickly moved along the passageway. All she could think of was to reach Bessel. She had no plans beyond that. He would know what to do, she decided . . .

Inside her flat Crane sat up as he heard the sound of her approaching footsteps. He picked up the gun from his lap and aimed it at the door, holding it with both hands. When she opened the door her body would be outlined by the light in the passageway, giving him a perfect target.

He heard the rattle of her keys as she took them out of her handbag.

Crane tensed.

Bessel was surprised when he found himself getting out of his car and running across the road. It was as if a part of him had come to a decision without informing his conscious mind. And yet he immediately knew he was doing the right thing, no matter what the consequences.

He raced through the front door and up the stairs. He had never moved so fast before in his life.

He started screaming her name as he bounded up the final flight.

'Roz! Don't go in there!'

He skidded round the corner and into the passageway that led to her flat. Relief flooded through him. At the end of the passageway stood Roz, frozen with surprise and her door key poised some inches from the lock. Her head was turned towards him, her eyes wide with surprise.

'Roz! Don't move!' he yelled as he ran.

'Jamie . . .' she began but never finished. A hole had

suddenly appeared in the door, spraying splinters into the air. Roz's body jerked and she gave a grunt of pain.

Her expression was a mixture of shock and incomprehension as the second bullet splintered the wood and hit her high in the chest, slamming her backwards into the wall behind her.

As her legs buckled and she started to slide down the wall she looked at Bessel imploringly, as if she hoped he would somehow make everything all right again. That's when the third bullet hit her. It struck her in the side of her lower jaw, tearing most of it away in an explosion of blood and fragments of bone.

She was still alive when Bessel reached her. He stood over her, staring down in horror. He'd seen shot people before but nothing as bad as this. Roz resembled something out of the worst of all possible nightmares. He wanted to scream.

The door to Roz's flat opened. He felt himself being roughly shoved aside. The next thing he knew Crane was bending over Roz, the gun in his hand. He placed the silenced muzzle against her temple . . .

The gun made a *phffd* sound and Roz gave a convulsive twitch and then was still.

Bessel couldn't take his eyes off her. Even when Crane shoved the bulbous silencer under his nose and he smelt the acrid fumes from it he kept staring at her.

A stinging slap across the face from Crane brought him out of his trance-like state. He turned his attention to Crane, and to the black hole in the end of the silencer.

'What the fuck were you playing at, Captain?' rasped Crane. 'Going soft like that at the last moment. Bad form, as you'd say, *sir*, really bad form . . .'

With a shock, Bessel suddenly realized that Crane intended to kill him too. Right there and then.

A door opened further along the passageway and a middle-aged man's startled face appeared. Crane turned and fired at him. The bullet missed but the man ducked his head back inside and slammed the door.

Bessel seized his chance. He turned and ran, zig-zagging as he went. He heard the *phffd* of Crane's gun again and pieces of plaster exploded from the wall just ahead of him but he kept going and reached the corner without being hit.

He literally flung himself down the stairs, ignoring the pain in his ribs as he slammed into the banisters. He was on the second landing when he heard the clatter of Crane's boots on the stairs overhead.

He jumped over the banister and landed heavily at the bottom of the stairwell. The impact sent a sharp pain shooting through his right ankle but the man-oeuvre had given him valuable seconds.

He rushed out into the night, hoping to reach his car. But as he ran across the road his injured ankle gave way beneath him and sent him pitching forward on his face.

Behind him he heard Crane run out of the building and onto the footpath. Dazed, he struggled to get up but he knew it was no good. He waited for the bullet slam into his back . . .

There was a screech of brakes, followed by the squeal made by rubber skidding over tarmac. Bessel looked and saw the front of a Jaguar looming over him. Its doors flew open and a man and a woman leapt out. For a moment he thought they were just an ordinary couple who just happened to be passing but the way they moved told him he was wrong. They had 'police' written all over them . . .

Crane obviously thought so too. Bessel heard the distinctive sound of the silenced gun being fired and one of the Jaguar's side windows shattered. As the man and the woman ducked Bessel got to his feet and ran . . .

*

Dempsey flung himself flat on the road as the man on the footpath fired again. He struggled to draw the Magnum, wondering at the same time if Makepeace was okay.

But then the gunman turned and began to sprint away down the street. Dempsey heard someone else running away as well. He jumped up and looked around. The other man – the one they'd almost hit with the car – was running up the street in the opposite direction. Makepeace, also getting to her feet, was looking back and forth between the two running men with indecision.

'You follow that one!' ordered Dempsey, pointing at the one he now recognized as Bessel. 'Take the car. I'll go after the other guy.'

Makepeace hesitated for a few seconds, knowing that Dempsey had chosen the more dangerous of the two for himself, but knowing there was no time to argue she nodded and leapt into the Jaguar.

By the time she got the car moving her quarry had reached the end of Abercorn Place and was turning right into Abbey Road.

She gunned the motor and sped up the street, then took the corner on two wheels, horn blaring to warn the oncoming traffic to get out of her way.

Bessel, despite a pronounced limp, was moving fast. He glanced back over his shoulder, saw the Jaguar mount the footpath behind him and put on a burst of speed. Then he ducked right down a side street.

Makepeace swore as she overshot the turning and had to stop and back up. She ignored the angry remonstrations of a bus driver who had had to swerve his vehicle across the road to avoid her.

She swung the Jaguar into the side street, peering ahead intently for her prey. Then she spotted him – running down the right-hand footpath. She sped after him.

He crossed an intersection and kept going straight

ahead. Makepeace was about to increase her speed but instead slammed her foot hard on the brake pedal. Her headlights had revealed something that Bessel hadn't seen. It wasn't a street but a short cul-de-sac.

The Jaguar skidded across the intersection and for a moment Makepeace thought she was going to lose control of the car and plough straight into a small post office on the corner. But to her relief the car slewed to a halt across the entrance to the cul-de-sac without hitting anything.

She got out quickly. Bessel was facing her with his back against the high wall that stretched between a pub on one side of the cul-de-sac and a garage on the other. Frantically he looked around for a way out but there wasn't one.

There were a few chairs and tables arranged in front of the pub, all shiny from a recent shower of rain. Bessel ran over and picked up one of the metal chairs. Then he began to advance menacingly on Makepeace, holding the chair over his head.

'I don't know who you are, bitch,' he said in a cracked voice, 'But you'd better get the hell out of my way or I'll brain you with this . . .'

'I'm a police officer and you're under arrest,' she told him. 'Put that chair down unless you want to make things even worse for yourself.'

The door of the pub opened and two men looked out. 'What's going on out here?' called one of them.

'Police business. Stay out of the way,' answered Makepeace calmly.

Bessel chose that moment of distraction to strike. He rushed at her, aiming the chair at her head. But the chair met nothing but empty air as Bessel swung it down – Makepeace had swiftly ducked to one side. Then, as the momentum of his attack brought him off balance, she slammed her elbow into the small of his back.

He and the chair hit the ground together. Makepeace

put her hands on her hips. 'Can we go now, or do you want to play some more?'

Groaning, Bessel got up, then unexpectedly lashed out at her with his right foot. It was a vicious kick aimed at her stomach but she simply took one step back and deftly caught hold of his foot. Then she yanked it upwards, giving it a sharp twist at the same time. There was a distinct crack and Bessel screamed.

He landed on his back, hard. This time he didn't get up again.

'Need any help, Miss?' It was one of the men standing in the pub doorway.

'No thank you,' said Makepeace. She walked back to her car and picked up the radio mike. Within seconds she was talking to Spikings. 'Chief? Harry. I've got Bessel . . .'

'What about Crane?'

'Dempsey was hot on his tail the last time I saw him. He should have him collared by now.' *I hope*, she added under her breath.

CHAPTER TEN

Dempsey was panting heavily by the time he reached the bottom of Abercorn Place. He hadn't shortened the gap between himself and the fleeing Crane by as much as an inch and he was forced to admit to himself that the keep-fit fanatic was probably in much better shape than he was.

Crane crossed Maida Vale and entered Elgin Avenue. As Dempsey followed him across the busy road, dodging the traffic, he suddenly realized what Crane had in mind when he spotted the distinctive red and blue sign of the London Underground up ahead on the left.

His lungs searing with every breath, Dempsey tried to increase his efforts but Crane remained the same distance ahead of him. Then, as he expected, he saw Crane disappear into the subway entrance.

There was no sign of Crane when Dempsey reached the top of the stairs leading down into the tube station. Dempsey paused to draw his gun and to suck in a deep breath then he headed down the stairs. He knew there was a good chance that Crane was waiting to ambush him but if he played it too cautious Crane would have the chance to hop on a train.

Dempsey landed at the bottom of the stairs in a crouch, the Magnum at the ready. But there was no sign of Crane. A young couple, standing at the ticket counter, were the only people around. They stared at him and the gun in alarm.

He pushed by them and ran through the ticket barrier, ignoring the yell from the ticket clerk. He arrived at the top of the escalator in time to see a man run out of view onto the south-bound platform. It had to be Crane . . .

Dempsey rushed down the escalator, taking several steps at a time. He was dreading that he'd hear the rumble of an approaching tube train.

A black woman, coming up on the ascending escalator, gave a shriek as she saw the gun in his hand. He reached the bottom, praying that the platforms wouldn't be crowded. What he needed was a clear shot.

His heart sank, however, as he ran onto the south-bound platform. There had obviously been a long time between trains and the place was packed with people.

He looked up and down the platform. He spotted a disturbance at one end. There were shouts of protest, then a woman screamed. Dempsey started to push his way through the crowd.

People were reluctant to move out of his way, even when he shouted he was a police officer. When they saw the Magnum, though, they moved much faster from his path.

But one heavily-built punk, sporting a mohawk haircut at least a foot long, deliberately blocked him, ignoring the gun.

'Why don't you push off, pig!' he sneered at Dempsey.

Dempsey didn't hesitate. He brought his right knee up hard into the punk's crotch then gave him a lightish rap across the head with the barrel of the Magnum as he started to fold.

After that people couldn't get out of his way fast enough.

Finally he was through the crowd. There was an empty space of about fifteen feet from there to the end of the platform and he immediately saw why.

Crane stood there by the mouth of the tunnel. He was holding a teenage girl in front of him, his arm around her neck. Pressed against the side of her face was the obscene bulge of a silencer.

'Back off!' cried Crane, his face ugly. 'Back off or I'll blow the top of her fucking head off!'

The girl, dressed in black jeans and leather jacket, was a study in pure terror. Her face was as white as bone and the black mascara around her eyes, made streaky by her tears, enhanced the skull-like effect.

Dempsey levelled the gun at Crane's head. 'You shoot her and I'll blow you all the way up the line to the next station,' he told Crane coldly.

'Are you crazy!' yelled Crane. 'I'm not kidding! I'll kill her unless you back off! So move!'

'You kill her and you got no hostage,' said Dempsey. 'It's stalemate, Crane. The only way you don't get a .44 bullet through your brains is if you let her go.'

Crane's face twisted with rage and rammed the silenced muzzle of the revolver hard into the girl's cheek. She made a sound that was a cross between a squeak and a whimper and shut her eyes.

'You got five seconds!' said Crane hoarsely. 'I count to five, cop, then I pull the trigger.'

'So count,' said Dempsey calmly, trying not to reveal the sick fear that was spreading upwards from the pit of his stomach.

Five seconds passed by. Long seconds. A flicker of confusion appeared in Crane's eyes. Then, with a snarl, he shoved the girl forward and, at the same time, swung the barrel of the gun towards Dempsey.

Dempsey, unable to fire because of the girl, flung himself down. He heard the muffled report from the .38 and felt something fizz through the air by his head. Behind him someone screamed . . .

As if watching a slow-motion movie Dempsey saw the girl fall on her face in front of him. He now had a clear field of fire and raised the Magnum . . . but Crane was already jumping from the platform . . .

Dempsey leapt up in time to see Crane disappear

into the black mouth of the tunnel. 'Stop or I fire!' he yelled but Crane kept going. Demsey aimed high and pulled the trigger. The .44 went off with an echoing boom. Then he ran to the end of the platform and jumped.

He almost overbalanced as he landed and for a moment he had an image of himself falling onto the live rail but he managed to keep upright. He entered the tunnel . . .

'Crane!' he yelled as he ran. 'Stop!' Then it occurred to him that with the lights of the station at his back he made a perfect target to Crane. He immediately moved to the side of the tunnel and ran as close to the wall as possible.

It was surprisingly dark in the tunnel. The illumination from the station didn't extend very far and very soon Dempsey couldn't see a thing. And when he looked behind him he found he couldn't even see the circle of light that marked the tunnel entrance. He realized that the tunnel had a curve to it – a relatively acute one.

He stopped and listened – trying to hear Crane's footsteps ahead of him over the sound of his own laboured breathing. But he couldn't hear anything . . .

He continued on but more slowly, feeling his way warily along the wall of the tunnel. He was certain that Crane was waiting for him in the darkness; waiting for him to come right up before he fired. Dempsey tried to be as quiet as possible.

Suddenly the wall disappeared and he stumbled sideways, making a loud noise. He discovered he'd fallen into a small alcove set in the tunnel wall, presumably as an emergency shelter for maintenance workers.

He was just about to step out of it when he heard a *phffd* sound close by and then the bullet ricochetting off the wall near to where he was.

Dempsey fired back blindly into the darkness. The

noise from the Magnum was deafening in the tunnel but in the flash from the barrel he got a brief glimpse of Crane some six yards away.

He fired again at where he'd seen Crane but this time the gun flash revealed Crane's back as he ran up the tunnel.

Dempsey left the protection of the alcove and gave chase. If he could catch up with Crane before the other man had the time to stop and aim again he could take him alive and keep Spikings happy . . .

The things I do for you, Chief, thought Dempsey as he ran blindly along the tunnel.

Then he came to an abrupt halt. He'd always thought the term 'his blood froze' was a piece of writer's hyperbole but at that moment he could actually feel a coldness sweeping through his body.

The cause was the gust of warm, stale air he felt against his face. It meant a tube train was approaching.

'Crane!' he called. 'There's a train coming! You've got to come back with me now. Drop your gun and hurry up . . . !'

There was silence for a few moments then Dempsey heard movement up ahead, followed by the familiar *phffd* sound of the silenced .38.

The bullet came nowhere near Dempsey. He raised the Magnum and prepared to fire. He could hear Crane coming quickly in his direction. And in the background he could hear the distant rumble of the train.

And then something remarkable happened . . .

There was a flash of blue light, a crackling sound followed by a high-pitched scream – and suddenly Dempsey could *see* Crane. He was outlined by the blue and white fire that formed a halo around his jerking, shuddering body; by the sparks that flew from his fingertips, his open mouth and from his hair which was standing bizarrely on end . . .

Crane, Dempsey realized, had blundered onto the live rail . . .

The screaming stopped and Crane, his clothes on fire, fell backwards. The only sound then was the sputter and sizzling of burning fats.

Then Dempsey became aware that the vibrations from the approaching train were much stronger now. He turned and began to run along the track as fast as he could.

He knew he had no chance of reaching the station before the train overtook him. All he could do was try and get to the alcove he'd been in before . . .

The trouble would be finding it again in the dark.

The roar of the hurtling train became deafening and the rush of warm air it was propelling ahead of it was like a strong wind. Dempsey had the horrible feeling that he wasn't going to make it.

He brushed his hand along the wall as he ran, hoping to feel the open space of the alcove but there was nothing but unyielding stonework.

He waited for the impact of the train, for the agony as the steel wheels did their appalling work on his body . . .

And then his extended fingers found empty space.

He hurled himself into the alcove, bruising his face against the wall as he did so.

Seconds later the train roared by – a crashing, metal monster of noise and streaks of bright light.

In the darkness that followed Dempsey let out a long sigh.

CHAPTER ELEVEN

Makepeace watched as Roz Carpenter's body, covered by a blood-stained sheet, was brought out on a stretcher by two uniformed policemen.

'So they used her, then they got rid of her,' she said bleakly to Spikings who was standing beside her. 'I wonder what the promise was – love or money?'

'Bit of both, according to Bessel,' answered Spikings. 'But I'd say it was more to do with love as far as she was concerned. She'd never been mixed up in anything even slightly shady before. Bessel charmed her into it, I reckon. You broke his leg, by the way.'

Makepeace shrugged. 'If I'd known about the girl it would have been his neck.'

'He says it was Crane who shot her – and that he was trying to save her.'

'Yeah, I'll bet,' she said sourly.

'Well, we'll know the full story when we talk to Crane . . .' Spikings turned and glowered down the road in the direction of Maida Vale tube station. 'Where the hell *is* Dempsey?'

At that moment a constable hurried up to Spikings. 'Excuse me, sir . . . we just got a radio message from the lads down at the tube station. They say a man's been killed – body's under the train . . .'

Makepeace gave an almost imperceptible gasp. She looked at Spikings and he saw that all the colour had drained from her face.

Quickly he said, 'It must be Crane. God knows Dempsey isn't the brightest thing on two legs but even he wouldn't be stupid enough to fall under a tube train.'

'I'm going down there . . .' said Makepeace firmly.

She headed towards her Jaguar but just as she reached it a white police car came speeding up the hill. It screeched to a stop behind one of the several other police vehicles parked in the street and a uniformed officer got out, followed by Dempsey. Dempsey looked a mess – his clothes and face covered in soot but he was obviously unharmed.

For an instant Spikings thought that Makepeace was going to go and fling herself on Dempsey but if that had been her intention, even momentarily, she quickly checked it. Instead she just stood there and said dryly, 'What happened, Dempsey? You get stuck up a chimney or something?'

Dempsey grimaced at her. 'Next time I'll take the easy one and *you* can go play in the subway.'

'Where's Crane?' asked Spikings.

'Splattered all over the Bakerloo line,' answered Dempsey, trying, unsuccessfully, to wipe some of the soot from his face with the back of his hand.

'What happened?'

'There was a bit of a shoot-out on the station platform. One woman got nicked by a stray bullet from Crane but she's okay. No bodies, apart from Crane's . . .'

'You shot him?' asked Spikings.

'*No*, sir,' said Dempsey, sounding aggrieved. 'You gave me orders not to shoot anyone, remember?'

'So what did happen to him?'

'He stood on a live rail. Went up like a 4th of July firework display. Then the train hit him . . .'

'Hell of a mess down there in the tunnel,' said the uniformed officer to Spikings. 'The LT engineers think it might be a whole day before they can repair the line.'

Spikings sighed. 'Be a lot less trouble – and cheaper – if you'd simply shot him, Dempsey.' He shook his head wearily, and added. 'I just can't win with you, can I, Yank?'

76

'Nossir.' He glanced at the ambulance that was just pulling away. 'What went on here? Where's Bessel?'

Makepeace told him briefly about Roz Carpenter, and her capture of Bessel.

'Nice work,' Dempsey told her.

'At least she got *her* man without bringing the London tube system to a halt,' growled Spikings.

'But . . .' Dempsey began to protest.

Spikings cut him off. 'I want a report on my desk in the morning. From the pair of you. And I want it bright and early.' He turned on his heel and headed for his car. Halfway there he paused, turned and said, grudgingly, 'I guess you two did okay.'

When he'd gone Dempsey grinned at Makepeace. 'Well, orders are orders. My place or yours?'

She raised her eyebrows. 'What on earth are you talking about?'

'You heard the man – we got to write a report together. So what's it to be – your place or mine?'

'You go to your place, I'll go to mine,' said Makepeace. 'I'll see you at the office tomorrow morning. If I have the time I may even take pity on you and translate your report into literate English before handing it in to the Chief. Night, Dempsey.'

She gave him a cool smile and walked off to her car. He stood watching her go, a wistful look on his face. 'See you, Wobblebum,' he murmured under his breath.

Then a thought struck him. His face brightened as he searched through his jacket pockets and extracted a piece of paper. There was a phone number written on it. Annabel's.

There were only three little girls splashing about together in the pool on this particular morning, but one of them was Ferris's daughter, Julie.

'Maybe she was a mermaid in a previous life,' said Dempsey quietly.

Ferris turned, surprised to see him. 'Hello, James. What brings you here this time?'

'Oh, I was just passing by and thought I'd drop in to see if you were here. I was curious to know if you've had any more visits from Mr Ottiano and his buddies.'

Ferris smiled. 'Haven't you heard? Ottiano has left the country. I'm sure we have you to thank for that. You put a scare into his British business associates. They got embarrassed and persuaded him it would be in everyone's interest if he made himself scarce.'

'Good. The guy's a maggot of the first order.'

'I even got that rise you swung for me. Not that I feel too happy about accepting it. I *should* have been a lot quicker on the uptake when it came to poor Roz . . .'

'I don't see how you could have been,' Dempsey told him. 'Unless you hire private eyes to follow all your girls how the hell are you going to know what they get up to out of working hours?'

'Yes, I suppose you're right.' He sighed. 'But what a shitty business it's all been. I liked Roz a lot. Damn that Bessel for getting her involved in the first place. I had her mother on the phone to me yesterday – ringing from Liverpool to ask me what the hell it was all about. She couldn't understand how it could have happened to *her* daughter. And, of course, I couldn't give her a satisfactory explanation.'

Dempsey nodded sympathetically, then said, 'But in your line of work trouble comes with the territory. Sooner or later.'

Ferris gave him a sharp look. 'What do you mean?'

'You know what I mean. I like a gamble myself and I like casinos but all that easy Big Money floating around attracts the flies and the maggots – on both sides of the table. Like Bessel and Ottiano. And when

78

the shit starts flying a lot of it ends up on innocent bystanders. You were lucky this time. Roz wasn't.'

Ferris nodded slowly.

'Maybe you *should* think seriously about getting into another line of business, like you told me you were.'

Ferris stared down at his daughter in the pool below and said thoughtfully, 'Dempsey, you may be right.'

CHAPTER TWELVE

'How'd you like to go to a wedding?'

Dempsey gave Annabel a suspicious stare. 'Is that a proposal?'

Annabel giggled. 'No, darling, it isn't. I'm afraid you're just not my father's type. Daddy would have a fit if I brought you home as husband material.'

'What's wrong with me?' asked Dempsey.

'As far as I'm concerned, not a thing, but in Daddy's eyes you would have three major failings. You're not upper class, you're not rich, and you're an American. Against those three handicaps the fact you're a marvellous fuck would mean very little to Daddy.'

Dempsey grinned and took another sip of coffee. They were sitting in Annabel's tiny kitchen in her expensive but small Chelsea flat. They were having breakfast, which for Dempsey consisted of black coffee and for Annabel white coffee and a single orange which she was in the process of peeling and cutting up into thin slivers. It was a kind of ritual with her every morning and Dempsey still found it fascinating to watch though he'd witnessed it several times now.

'Whose wedding is it then?' he asked.

'Sarah Hackett's. A schoolfriend of mine. And of Harriet's too. So she'll be there.'

'Oh yeah?' said Dempsey, more interested now.

Annabel finished the dissection of the orange and put the small, sharp knife down on the wooden cutting board. She gave Dempsey a knowing look. 'You really do have a thing about our dear Harry, don't you?'

'I wouldn't say that,' he answered uncomfortably.

'Hey, don't think I mind or anything,' she told him.

'Our relationship is perfectly straightforward and that's how I like it. I'm not after anything else from you so don't think I'm jealous. I'm just curious about you two.'

Dempsey looked at her. She was sitting across the narrow table wearing nothing but his shirt, which she had, as usual, neglected to button. With her long black hair, high cheek bones and striking eyes she was a very attractive woman and he enjoyed her company, both in and out of bed, but he had to admit to himself he would have preferred to be facing Makepeace across that breakfast table. Though knowing her the shirt would probably be buttoned up . . .

'There's nothing to be curious about,' he said finally. 'There's nothing between us at all apart from our work.'

'But you'd like there to be?' she persisted.

He shrugged. 'Eat your orange before it gets cold. And tell me about this Sarah dame.'

Seeing that she wasn't going to get anything else from him Annabel sighed and said, 'Sarah was the school virgin. Very sweet girl and everyone liked her but she was a total innocent when it came to sex. Determined to keep herself pure and all that. And from all accounts has continued to do so, until now. It's all due to her father in my view.'

'Her father?'

'You've probably heard of him. Judge Hackett. Or "Hackett the Hatchet" as the popular papers call him. Very strict in the Old Testament manner. An eye for an eye, and an arm and a leg as well for good measure. When they abolished capital punishment in this country it was the blackest day of his life.'

'Yeah,' said Dempsey. 'I have read about him. There was a controversy just a couple of weeks ago about one of his sentences being incredibly harsh . . .'

Annabel nodded. 'Well, he was just as strict with poor Sarah. Talk about a Victorian Puritan — he'd filled her head with all kinds of rubbish about sex, and everything else. I used to feel really sorry for her. She was terrified of him but would never even think of disobeying him about anything.'

'What about her mother?'

'She died when Sarah was only three so the Judge raised her by himself, unfortunately. I'm astonished the old bastard has given his approval for the marriage but then the husband-to-be sounds just like the sort of clot he *would* approve of.'

'Who is he?' asked Dempsey.

'His name is Richard Stradling. He's a rising young Tory MP. Used to be a solicitor. Very strong on law and order issues, especially anything to do with censorship. Big supporter of the video censorship bill and now wants the same sort of censorship rules applied to films and television. He's a lay preacher as well—' Annabel smirked. '—though he doesn't look as if he's capable of laying anything.'

'Sounds like you aren't exactly crazy about him. Have you met him?'

'Only once. At a cocktail party at his London flat. The first thing he told me was that he didn't allow smoking in the place. He doesn't drink either. He's not bad looking in a wet sort of way but he seems the sort who'd be happier leading a troop of boy scouts on a ramble than going to bed with a woman. God knows what Sarah sees in him, unless perhaps he's hung like a carthorse.'

'Annabel,' said Dempsey sternly. 'You have a one-track mind.'

She ate the last sliver of her orange and licked her lips delicately. Then she said, 'Are you complaining?'

'Are you kidding?'

She leaned forward on the table. The shirt fell open. 'Are you in any particular rush this morning . . . ?'

Dempsey was about to shake his head but then he thought to glance at his watch. He frowned when he saw the time. 'Shit, I've got to meet Harry at the Reading police station at 11.30 to tie up some loose ends on a case out there. I'd better get moving soon if I'm going to be there on time.'

'Rats,' she muttered, sitting back in her chair.

He finished his coffee quickly. 'So when is this wedding?'

'Next Saturday. Interested in being my escort?'

'Yeah. Why not. Be fun to see the look on Harry's face when I make an appearance.'

'Yes, I'll probably die laughing,' said Annabel sourly. She stood up and removed his shirt. 'Here,' she said, handing it to him. 'You may need this . . .'

'Thanks again for coming down this weekend, Harriet. It was very sweet of you. I'm sure there must have been a hundred things you would rather have done.'

'Sarah, if I'm going to be your Matron of Honour when you get spliced next Saturday the very least I could have done was to have met the groom,' said Makepeace with a conviction she didn't feel. In reality the weekend had been a bore for her.

They were driving along a country lane that led towards Pangley, a small town north-west of Reading. It was a beautiful morning but for some reason Makepeace felt oddly depressed. She guessed that the previous two days had something to do with her mood.

'What did you think of Richard?' asked Sarah.

Was it her imagination, Makepeace wondered, or had she detected a note of anxiousness in Sarah's voice. She glanced at her friend and wished yet again she had the courage of her convictions. All during the weekend she had wanted to take Sarah aside somewhere and say, Sarah, are you sure you want to go through with this? Is it really what you want? But she hadn't . . .

Probably because she knew what the answer would have been. Sarah would have stared at her in surprise and said, 'But of *course* it is, Harriet!' And Makepeace would know that once again, as usual, Sarah would be echoing her father's wishes instead of her own. For years now Makepeace had been trying in vain to persuade Sarah to start thinking for herself rather than acting as her father's puppet but all her efforts had been in vain and she'd finally given up. She suspected it was too late for Sarah to change now.

'I think Richard's very nice,' she told Sarah, lying through her teeth.

'I'm glad,' said Sarah, though she didn't sound very glad.

This encouraged Makepeace to say, 'But I must say I did find him a little too, er, *serious* about things.'

'He's a very serious man, especially about his work,' said Sarah defensively.

'Fine, but does he ever relax and let his hair down a bit?' asked Makepeace. 'Does he ever have any *fun*?'

'Richard says the time for relaxation will come when he's achieved his goal and saved the children of this country from the corrupting influence of television. He won't rest until that day.'

Give me strength, thought Makepeace. Aloud she said, 'I gathered from our conversations that he tended to blame TV and videos for most of what's wrong in Britain.'

Sarah nodded. 'Yes, he does.'

'Don't you think that's, ah, a little *extreme*?'

'Oh no. He's got the statistics to prove it. I'm sure he'd be happy to show them to you. Shall I ask him?'

'Er, don't bother,' said Makepeace quickly. 'Apart from his TV campaign he's got other political ambitions, hasn't he?'

'Oh yes. He hopes to be Home Secretary some day. Just think, Harriet, when he becomes Home Secretary he'll be your boss, in a way.'

'What a jolly thought,' said Makepeace.

'Of course, that's if you're still in the police force by then.'

'Why shouldn't I be?'

'Well, you might get married in the meantime.'

'I sincerely hope not. But even if I did get married I wouldn't give up my job.'

'What if you had children?'

'Please, not while I'm driving . . .'

'Don't you like children?' asked Sarah, surprised.

'Other people's, in small doses. What about you?'

'Oh, Richard wants a large family. But I must admit I'm a little frightened by childbirth itself. Though I expect once you have the first one the others are much easier.'

Makepeace gave her a sympathetic glance but said nothing. There was nothing she could say.

The car was just entering Pangley's main street. The railway station was situated at the other end of it. 'Are you sure I can't give you lift all the way to London. This business I've got with the Reading boys won't take long.'

'No, it's okay,' said Sarah. 'I must take this train. Daddy's meeting me at the other end and giving me lunch before I go to Harrods . . . *oh* . . .'

She gasped as Makepeace, turning into the station car park, narrowly avoided hitting a man who had run in front of the car. Makepeace had had to swerve violently to miss him. 'Idiot!' she yelled as they went by.

The man, shabbily dressed and in his early thirties, turned and stared expressionlessly at them.

'Sorry about that,' said Makepeace to Sarah as she pulled up in front of the station entrance.

'It's okay. It would have been awful if you'd hit him.' She opened the door and got out. 'Thanks for the lift, Harriet. See you later in the week.' She shut the door.

Makepeace leaned over and wound down the passenger window. 'Listen – I'll ring you tomorrow and I'll be down again on Friday night. Take care, darling.'

Sarah smiled at her. 'You too, Harriet.'

'What are you buying in Harrods, by the way?' asked Makepeace.

'Oh! Linen and things.'

'Linen?'

'Bed linen. You know . . .' said Sarah awkwardly. Then, 'Must dash or I'll miss my train. See you next Friday.'

Makepeace watched her hurry towards the station entrance, a worried smile on her face. Sarah was an attractive woman – slim, with ash blonde hair and blue eyes – but there was a nervous vulnerability about her that always made Makepeace anxious on her behalf. She winced as she saw Sarah bump into a man in the doorway, mutter an apology and disappear inside.

Makepeace sighed and wound the window up. She looked at her reflection in the rear-view mirror and said, 'I need this wedding like a hole in the head.' Then she drove away.

As she stood in the ticket queue Sarah didn't notice that the man immediately behind her was the one Makepeace had almost run down. And she was also too preoccupied to notice that he was staring at her in a fixed, unnerving manner. He had an odd face. It was very thin with an elongated lower jaw. It was also asymmetrical with the features of one side lower than the other. It had the effect of making it look as if one half of his face was melting . . .

Sarah bought her ticket and headed for the door leading to the platform. At the doorway she collided with the same middle-aged businessman she'd collided with coming into the station. She apologized to him for the second time and hurried on.

The thin-faced man followed her.

He stood a short distance behind her on the platform and continued to stare intently at her. But now there was blatant hunger in his gaze.

CHAPTER THIRTEEN

Sir Lionel Hackett stood by the barrier at platform 8 and watched as his daughter's train pulled slowly into Paddington Station. Though sixty-four years old he looked ten years younger and held his tall, slim body very straight and erect. He had a long, angular face with a grey, military style moustache and fierce blue eyes. Over six feet two inches tall there was an aura of power about him and people instinctively gave him a wide berth as he stood there in his long, black overcoat, an old-fashioned, silver-topped walking stick hooked over one arm.

A slight frown appeared on his face as the passengers alighted from the train and began to file past him through the barrier. He could see no sign of Sarah.

The frown deepened by the time there were only a few stragglers left on the platform and it was obvious his daughter wasn't on the train. The silly girl, he decided, had missed it. It wasn't like her to be so careless. She knew how valuable his time was.

He was about to go and see when the next train was due when he saw one of the train guards, who'd been walking along the platform and checking the carriages, suddenly stop beside one of the nearby First Class carriages and peer in through one of the windows with a look of alarm on his face. Then the guard tore open the compartment door and climbed inside . . .

Almost immediately he re-emerged, hand clamped over his mouth. Then he turned and ran towards the barrier.

Filled with a sick certainty that something terrible had happened, Sir Lionel ran onto the platform, passing the guard who didn't even notice him.

Somehow Sir Lionel knew what he was going to find in the compartment even before he got there but even so that didn't lessen the shock.

Sarah lay there on the compartment floor. She was naked from the waist down. And she was covered in blood.

Her throat had been cut.

Makepeace didn't conceal her disapproval as she watched Dempsey consume his third consecutive cheeseburger. 'Do you always take a brace of those things?' she asked.

'Only in the open season,' he said with a full mouth.

'Is there ever a closed season with you?'

'No.' He finished the hamburger and wiped the tomato sauce from his mouth with a paper napkin. 'Not bad, for a Brit hamburger. Almost like the real thing.'

They were sitting in a hamburger bar in Reading. Dempsey had insisted on having something to eat before they began the journey back to London. 'I think I might even have another one,' he said, and clicked his fingers at the waitress. She came over looking surly. Dempsey ordered his fourth hamburger then turned to Makepeace. 'You sure you don't want anything?'

She sighed. 'Oh very well.' To the waitress she said, 'Could I have some lemon tea, please?'

'Do what?' said the waitress, a girl in her late teens who obviously didn't have her heart and soul in her profession.

'Lemon tea,' repeated Makepeace. Then added in a patronizing tone, 'It's tea with just a thin slice of lemon floating gently on the surface. Could you possibly manage that?'

Unimpressed, the girl said, 'I'll have to charge you extra for the lemon.'

'That's all right,' said Makepeace coldly. 'My friend here will pay.'

The girl sniffed and slouched off. Makepeace watched her go and then said to Dempsey, 'Vivacious little creature, isn't she?'

Dempsey grinned. 'You're sure in a mean mood today. What's wrong?'

'Oh, nothing in particular. It's just that I had a very dull weekend. With an old friend of mine and her husband-to-be. They're getting married next week-end . . .'

'Yeah, Sarah Hackett. Judge Hackett's daughter,' said Dempsey.

She looked at him in surprise. 'How did you . . . ?' she began, but then understanding dawned in her eyes. 'Oh . . . you're still seeing Annabel. She must have told you.'

Dempsey took a sip of coffee and nodded.

'And how is dear Annabel?'

'In pretty good shape. In *very* good shape, come to think of it . . .'

Makepeace held up a hand. 'Please, spare me the gruesome details. I'll take your word for it.'

'So why was your weekend so dull?'

'It consisted mainly of listening to lectures from her fiancé about the moral decline of the country and what he proposes to do about it.'

'From Annabel's description of him the guy sounds like a total nerd.'

'I'm not sure what that means but it sounds a suitable description. And he's also straight-laced to the point of absurdity. I feel so sorry for Sarah. She's making a big mistake but there's nothing I can do about it. She's a lovely girl but she's such a wimp. She's swapping one leash for another.'

'Leash?'

'The one her father's had round her neck all her life.' Makepeace shook her head sadly.

'I hear the Judge is a real tough old guy. Especially behind the bench.'

'Too tough. I'm against lenient sentences myself but some of his judgements have been absurd. Like the woman he sent to prison for five years on a shop-lifting charge.'

'Do you know him well?'

'I haven't seen him since I was a schoolgirl. I went to stay at Sarah's once during a school holiday. Once was enough. Life with the judge made boarding school seem like heaven. Talk about *strict*! I must admit I was rather relieved he was too busy to come down from London this weekend . . .'

'Well, you'll have to see him next Saturday.'

'Don't remind me,' she said wearily. 'Why I ever agreed to be Sarah's matron of honour I'll never know.'

'Matron of *what*?'

'Quite. It's a sort of whipper-in for a covey of nasty little bridesmaids and pageboys – who in this case will probably turn out to be the local beaver troop and a gaggle of brownies.'

Dempsey looked blankly at her. At that moment his hamburger arrived, and Makepeace's tea. 'Well, I'm sure you know what you're talking about.' He picked up the cheeseburger in both hands and took a large bite out of it. Tomato sauce and juice trickled from between the buns. Makepeace winced.

'I wish you wouldn't do that,' she said.

'What?'

'Eat that way. You may have noticed the knife and fork by your plate.'

Dempsey took another bite from the cheeseburger. 'You don't eat a hamburger with a knife and fork,' he told her as he chewed.

'Yes, you can. Eating that way is just another of your annoying American habits, like clicking your fingers at the waitress.'

'I can't help acting like an American, princess. I *am* an American.'

'That fact is painfully obvious but you're in England now and it's about time you adopted the English way of doing things.'

He nodded. 'Whatever you say, princess.' Then he peered into her cup and said, 'Is that the English way of drinking lemon tea? With milk in it?'

She looked down, saw that there *was* milk in her lemon tea and scowled. Dempsey sniggered. She glared at him but said nothing.

'Hey, we'd better get moving pretty soon or we'll be late for the Chief's meeting and he'll chew our asses off,' he told her, glancing at the clock on the wall. 'Better hurry up and drink your tea.'

'I don't want it,' she said stonily.

'I'll get the check then.' He raised his hand and clicked his fingers at the waitress.

Sir Lionel stood looking out of the plate glass window of the Station Master's office. The window offered an overhead view of the entire station but all he could see was his daughter's mutilated body lying on the floor of the compartment.

There were two plain clothes detectives in the office with him, both watching him with concerned expressions. Finally the older of the two officers, Detective Inspector Wilson of the Flying Squad, stepped forward and said hesitantly, 'I don't think there's any need to detain you, my Lord – if perhaps I could have a very brief and informal statement then we can . . .'

'No you may not,' snapped Sir Lionel without turning from the window.

Startled, Wilson said, 'Beg pardon, my Lord?'

'I said, Inspector Wilson, you may *not*.' He turned from the window. There were tears streaming down his face but his voice was steady. 'You may not have a statement. Furthermore you will not remove my daughter's body from that train, nor will any more be done at all until Chief Superintendent Spikings is here and has personally taken charge of this case.'

Wilson stared at him blankly. 'I'm sorry, sir, I don't quite follow . . .'

'Then let me spell it out for you, Wilson,' said Sir Lionel, his blue eyes glittering with tears. 'Unless I get Spikings here, and bloody fast, then the Home Secretary will be asking for your resignation.'

Less than forty-five minutes later Sir Lionel and Spikings were walking down the platform towards the screens that had been erected around the compartment that contained Sarah Hackett's body.

'Our time in Malaya seems a long way off, sir,' said Spikings, his voice deferential.

'Yes . . . yes,' answered the Judge very softly. 'A long way off . . .'

'Out of one jungle into another, eh, sir?'

'I preferred the Malayan one. It was cleaner.' He stopped and turned, fixing Spikings with his fierce blue eyes. 'I saved your life once, remember?'

'Yes, of course I do, sir. How could I forget . . . ?'

'You told me you'd be forever in my debt.'

'Yessir,' said Spikings worriedly. 'And I meant it.'

'Good. Because I'm going to ask a favour of you, Gordon. An important one.'

'Yessir?'

'I want you to find my daughter's killer. And find him quickly . . . Before I do.'

CHAPTER FOURTEEN

Dempsey and Makepeace crept into the briefing room at S.I.10 headquarters like two school children late for class. Both carrying paper cups of coffee, they squeezed along the back row and sat down in two vacant seats. Dempsey looked at his watch and frowned. 'The Chief's not here yet. I was sure we'd be late . . .'

'He was held up by some flap at a railway station,' explained the officer sitting next to Dempsey. 'No idea yet what it was all about but the request for his presence came from the top level apparently . . .'

At that moment Spikings strode into the room. Never a cheerful-looking man at the best of times he appeared unusually grim today, Dempsey noticed. *Uh oh*, thought Dempsey, *I smell trouble* . . .

'There's been a change of schedule,' Spikings announced to the assembled S.I.10 officers. 'I know this meeting was supposed to have been about the Heathrow bullion job but something else has come up . . .'

He ignored the puzzled murmur that this announcement produced and continued: 'Earlier today a young woman was raped and murdered. Multiple stab wounds were inflicted upon her body during the struggle and then her throat was cut. The preliminary medical examination has put the time of death at approximately 11.20 am. The incident took place in one of the first class compartments of the train from Bristol to Paddington and the time of death indicates that the train was somewhere between Reading and Slough . . .'

Dempsey suddenly felt uneasy. He glanced at Make-peace and saw that she was frowning. His uneasiness increased.

Spikings went on, 'After Slough the train stopped only once. At Ealing Broadway, so the killer could have got off at either Slough, Ealing Broadway or, if he had enough bottle – Paddington. Trouble is he should have been easy to spot. No way he could have avoided getting blood on his clothes but no one remembers seeing anyone with blood-stained clothes at any of those stations.

'The body was discovered by a guard at Paddington. And now we come to the best bit – the victim's father was waiting at the station to meet her and was one of the first to see the body. Her father is none other than Sir Lionel Hackett . . .'

Dempsey heard Makepeace's stifled gasp. He saw tears start to roll down her face.

'Jesus, kid . . .' he whispered, giving her arm a squeeze. She continued to stare straight ahead, head erect but she was obviously fighting to keep control.

'Two hours ago,' said Spikings, 'I received a phone call from the Home Secretary – Sir Lionel, it appears, has insisted that this department handle the bulk of the investigation, and to that end we will put all other activities on the back burner. There are reasons for Sir Lionel's request I won't go into them now . . .'

'As the situation stands at the moment we have nothing to go on. No witnesses, no fingerprints, and no other information until after the autopsy. The Coroner's Inquest is already in session – the law doesn't hang about for one of its own and the autopsy should take place later this afternoon . . .'

Makepeace was trembling now. Dempsey gently took the cup from her hand and set it down on the floor. 'C'mon, kid, let's get some air.'

He helped her stand and guided her along the row towards the door.

Spikings had dried up in mid-flow. He stared at them in amazement, his face darkening with anger. Then he cried, 'Where the *hell* do you think you two are going? This meeting isn't over yet!'

'We'll be back with you guys in a couple of minutes,' Dempsey told him.

'You *what*?' roared Spikings. 'Sit down immediately or I'll put you both on suspension!'

Dempsey, his hands on Makepeace's shoulders, stopped and turned to Spikings. 'Chief,' he said very quietly but very clearly, 'Unless you want to wear your teeth on a string for the rest of your life you'd better back off . . .'

There was a stunned silence in the room. Several of the officers seemed to be trying to shrink into their clothes. Spikings' mouth gaped open in shocked surprise and his face went even darker. But the expected explosion never came, because then he seemed to notice that there was something wrong with Makepeace . . .

As the silence in the room continued Dempsey calmly ushered Makepeace outside and shut the door behind him.

He led her over to a bench seat and sat her down. She put her face in her hands and started to silently cry, her shoulders shaking violently.

Dempsey sat down beside her. He waited patiently for her to get the worst of it out of her system and then, when her sobbing began to subside, took a hip flask out of his jacket and held it in front of her.

'Here, drink this,' he told her. 'Top quality bourbon. Do you good.'

She hesitated then accepted the flask. She took several long swallows and then, coughing, handed the flask back to him. 'Thanks, Dempsey,' she gasped.

A door opened. Dempsey looked up and saw Spikings approaching. He looked calmer now but still angry. He frowned when he saw the state Makepeace was in and said, as calmly as he could, to Dempsey, 'What the hell is going on? What's the matter with Harry?'

'She spent the weekend with the Judge's daughter. She's an old friend of Harry's. And who was it who put her on the train this morning? Harry, that's who . . .'

'Oh shit,' said Spikings softly.

'I *told* her I'd give her a lift all the way to London,' said Makepeace in a strangled voice. 'But she said no. She had to meet her damned father. I should have insisted . . .'

'Easy, Harry,' said Spikings, uncomfortably. Then, 'Do you want to go home?'

She shook her head firmly. 'No. I've got work to do. I'm going to get Sarah's killer.'

Spikings looked at Dempsey. Dempsey gave a slight shrug. Spikings had one more try. 'Harry, I really think you should take the rest of the day off. You've had a bad shock.'

'I'll be all right,' she said. 'Just give me a few minutes . . .'

'Chief! Telephone!' It was Chas Jarvis, Spikings' deputy, calling from the doorway of his office. Spikings glared at him. 'I'm not available!' he snapped. 'Tell whoever it is I'm in conference or something . . .'

'It's the Coroner's office. Says it's important,' said Jarvis.

Spikings muttered an obscenity under his breath and went off to take the call. When he'd gone Dempsey said, 'You sure you want to hang around here?'

'Yes,' said Makepeace, looking him straight in the eye. 'I owe it to Sarah. I was one of the last people to see her alive, which means it's important that I get to work on the case as soon as possible while my memory is still fresh.'

Dempsey nodded. 'Yeah, you're right. *Can* you

remember anything about dropping her off at the station?'

'No. I just drove up, she got out of the car and I drove off . . .' Makepeace took a Kleenex out of her handbag and blew her nose. 'Do you know what she told me over breakfast this morning? That she was worried about her wedding night. She was still a virgin, you see . . . Oh God, I just can't believe it happened! Not to Sarah . . . it would be bad enough for anyone else to die that way but for it to have happened to her is somehow *worse* . . . it just *shouldn't* have happened!'

Dempsey squeezed her shoulder. 'Easy princess. Try and concentrate on what you saw when you dropped her off. Remember as much about it as you can. Picture it in your mind . . . run it over and over like a movie . . .'

'Oh, Dempsey,' said Makepeace, irritated. 'Don't give me all that old police cadet school crap . . .' She paused suddenly and frowned.

'You okay?' asked Dempsey.

'Shut up,' she said, blinking rapidly. Then, slowly, she said, 'I think I *do* remember some . . .'

They were both startled by a door being slammed very loudly. It was Spikings. He looked furious as he came along the corridor.

'Now what?' asked Dempsey.

'Sir Lionel has stuck his oar in where it's not needed,' growled Spikings. 'And by doing so has left us up the proverbial shit creek without a paddle.'

'What do you mean?' asked Makepeace.

'His Lordship has bent the ear of his good mate the Chief Constable who in turn has got hold of the coroner and put the block on the autopsy.'

'What? *Why*?' cried Makepeace.

'Because he doesn't want her "got at" anymore – that's why.' Dempsey shook his head in disgust. 'I'll

98

have a go at trying to make him change his mind myself but knowing how stubborn he can be I'm afraid it will be a waste of time.'

'I just hope that the forensic lads can get some info from the carriage and her clothes otherwise we're in big trouble.'

CHAPTER FIFTEEN

The girl sat in front of the console with a thick data book open on her lap. There was the outline of a face on the screen – a man's face. It was thin and oddly misshapen.

Behind the girl stood Dempsey and Makepeace. Makepeace was frowning with concentration. 'It's so difficult,' she said, 'I only had a brief glimpse of him through the windshield.'

'You're doing fine,' Dempsey told her.

She sighed. 'Now I know what all those witnesses I've questioned over the years felt like.' She stared at the screen and then said, 'His hair was longer, I think. And his face was a bit thinner. Sort of pinched.'

The girl consulted her data book and then tapped in more figures, her fingers flying over the keyboard with consummate skill. The face on the screen changed . . .

Makepeace regarded it carefully. 'It's close but it's not exactly right. Can you make his eyes narrower? They kind of drooped in the corners . . .'

Again the girl's fingers flew over the keyboard and again the face on the screen changed.

'Yes,' said Makepeace. 'That's a lot better.'

The door was suddenly flung open and Spikings strode into the small office with Jarvis hard on his heels. 'Well?' he demanded. 'How's it coming?'

Makepeace pointed at the screen. 'That's pretty close to the man I saw at the station. Not exactly right but good enough.'

Spikings peered at the face. 'Fine,' he grunted. 'We'll use it . . .'

'But Chief, like I told you, all that happened was that I nearly knocked him down with my car . . .'

'Yeah, and you noticed something strange about him too, you said.'

'Only that he acted a bit odd. He didn't react in a normal way. He just stared as we went by . . .'

'Well, as far as I'm concerned that's enough reason to follow it up. I know it isn't much to go on but at the moment it's the nearest thing to a lead we've got.' He turned to Jarvis. 'I want copies of that picture featured in the news programmes of all four TV channels tonight without fail. You have any trouble from any of the producers you tell me. I'll fall on them like a ton of bricks. Send out copies to all the papers as well . . .' He turned back to Makepeace. 'As for you, I'm afraid I've got a somewhat dirty job I want you to do.'

'What is it?'

'I tried to talk Sir Lionel into changing his mind about the autopsy on his daughter but I got nowhere with him. So now I want you to have a go. You were a friend of Sarah's – he might listen to you.'

Makepeace's face stiffened. 'I'd rather not see him, sir.'

'What you'd *rather* do doesn't concern me, Sergeant!' barked Spikings, making her flinch. 'What I'm *ordering* you to do is go talk to Sir Lionel and try and make him change his mind. You do *have* an interest in finding his daughter's murderer, don't you?'

'Yessir,' she answered in a subdued voice. 'Of course, sir.'

'Then *move*, dammit!'

She moved.

John Bates opened the door of his battered mini and almost fell into the street. Hanging onto the side of the car door he managed to save himself, then unfolded the rest of his long body out of the small car. He slammed the door then stood there swaying in the street.

He staggered across the footpath and then up to the front door of the tiny terraced house. He fumbled, unsuccessfully, in his pocket for a while and then pressed the doorbell. When that produced no immediate response he began to rap the door-knocker as well.

He stopped only when he was aware that the door was being unlocked. It opened a short way, a thick length of chain preventing it from going any further. The old woman peered hard at him but there was no recognition on her face. 'Who is it?' she demanded.

'It's *me*, Mum!' cried Bates in a slurred voice. 'For Christ sakes, let us in . . . I can't find me fucking key . . .'

'Don't swear! I will not have it in this house!' she snapped.

'I'm not in the bloody house, am I? And I won't be unless you open the damn door.'

'You're drunk!' she said accusingly. 'You're drunk and it's not past 7 o'clock yet.'

'Mum, open the door, will you?'

Mrs Bates unchained the door. Her son lurched past her into the hallway, almost falling over. She shut the door and followed after him.

'Look at the state of you – have you been driving your car like that?' she cried.

'I'm all right! Just don't start on me!'

'One of these days you're going to kill someone driving in that state. If your father was alive he'd knock some sense into you.'

'He knocked you about enough times but it never made you any smarter, did it?'

The old woman looked stricken. 'I won't have you running down your father, do you hear? I won't! He was a good man, he was!'

'Oh yeah, he was bloody great,' sneered Bates. 'The bastard . . .'

He started to climb the stairs but she grabbed hold

102

of his arm. 'John! You're not going anywhere until you say you're sorry for what you said about your Dad!'

He shook himself free of her hand and continued up the stairs, holding onto the banister to keep his balance. 'Leave me alone,' he groaned. 'I don't feel well . . .'

'John! Come back down here!'

But he ignored her. He staggered into his room and slammed the door. Then he collapsed heavily onto his sagging, single bed.

He waited, with his eyes closed, for everything to stop spinning. His stomach was queasy and his face felt clammy. He hoped he wasn't going to throw up.

But after a few minutes the nausea passed and he opened his eyes. He surveyed the familiar surroundings of the room he'd lived in for over thirty years. He hated the room but at the same time appreciated the feeling of security it gave him.

His eyes fixed on the wall covered with nude pin-ups, all of them explicit to a degree that was almost medical. His mother disapproved but had given up tearing them down as he only replaced them right away.

He began to feel sexually aroused. He sat up and reached for the pile of magazines beside his bed. He opened one at random, then unzipped his fly . . .

Afterwards he dozed for a while then woke up feeling hungry. He got up and went downstairs. The door to the front room was shut and he could hear the sound of the TV coming from inside. It was turned up loud because of his mother's increasing deafness. He hoped she wouldn't hear him go past – he couldn't take any more of her tonight.

But just as he was about to enter the kitchen he heard her cry out. Then the door to the front room flew open and she rushed out. She was about to go up the stairs but stopped when she saw him standing in the hallway. 'John!' she cried. 'What have you done? What have you done now . . . ?'

He frowned at her, disturbed by the expression on her face. 'What are you on about?' he demanded.

She gestured frantically at him. 'Come and see this! Just you come and see this!' She turned and pointed at the TV set. 'Quickly!'

Worried, he went and pushed by her into the front room. What he saw on the television screen shocked him . . .

It was his face.

An imperfect reproduction, true, but unmistakably his face.

Then he became aware of what the announcer was saying: '. . . according to the police the rape and murder of the daughter of Sir Lionel Hackett, the High Court judge, was a particularly brutal and vicious one. They are anxious to interview this man who was seen acting suspiciously in the vicinity of Pangley Station shortly before the victim caught her train to London. If you recognize this man please call the following number immediately . . .'

Bates' face vanished from the screen and was replaced by a London phone number.

He felt his mother grab him by the arm. 'You've finally done it, haven't you! You dirty, wicked man . . . !'

He tried to get away from her but she clung onto him. 'Leave it, will you!' he shouted. 'It's nothing to do with me!'

'It must be, else why would the police have your picture?!' she yelled. 'You killed her! Not satisfied with exposing yourself to decent folk you've bloody well topped someone now! I should have known this would happen sooner or later, you filthy pervert!'

'Shut up! Shut up, you silly old bag!' he cried, struggling with her. 'I didn't do nothing to her! I swear it!'

'Don't lie!' I know you did it! And to the judge's

104

daughter too! He knows you! Your poor father worked for that man for years . . .'

'Will you let *go* of me! I didn't touch her!'

'I knew you weren't right in the head from the word go!' she screamed at him. 'I should have put a pillow over your face when you was a baby, you dirty no-good . . .'

Bates shoved her away as hard as he could. She gave a cry of alarm as she lost her grip on his arm and fell backwards, her hands fluttering . . .

There was a sickening *thonk* as her head struck the corner of the TV set and then she landed on the floor like a dummy full of saw-dust. She lay there completely still.

For nearly half a minute Bates just stood there looking down at her in silence. 'Mum . . . ?' he said finally. 'Mum? You all right?'

There was no response. Reluctantly he went over to her and bent down. She lay on her back with her head turned to one side. He reached down and turned her face towards him. Then he gasped.

Her eyes were half open but only the whites showed. Thick blood oozed out of a horribly deep gash on her temple, and a trickle of saliva ran from the corner of her mouth.

'Mum?' he said softly. By his head the TV set continued to blare out its news bulletin. The commentator was now saying something about a threatened postal strike. Bates turned it off. The silence that followed was unnerving. Bates tried to detect some sign of life in his mother but couldn't. She wasn't breathing. He had to face the unthinkable. She was dead . . . and he had killed her.

He stood up and backed away from her body. Then he went to the sideboard and opened it. There was just one bottle inside. Sweet sherry. It was three-quarters full. It was his mother's.

He drank half of it in one go, then carried the bottle

105

with him into the kitchen where he got down an old biscuit tin from a high shelf. The tin contained nine single pound notes and a lot of change in silver. He put the lot in his pockets, then he finished the sherry and headed for the front door.

As he opened the front door he suddenly paused. The image of his face on the TV screen flashed through his mind. He shut the door again and ran upstairs to the bathroom. He found a small pair of scissors and began to snip clumsily at his hair.

When he'd finished his longish hair had been reduced to an untidy stubble of varying lengths. It didn't really make his unique features any less noticeable but Bates felt confident he had drastically altered his appearance.

He started down the stairs when he remembered something else; he retraced his steps, hurried into his bedroom and picked up his jacket from the floor where he'd thrown it earlier.

On the way out he decided, reluctantly, to check his mother again. He looked into the front room. She was lying in exactly the same position as he'd last seen her. And she was just as motionless as before.

He gave a deep sigh and then left the house. Outside, as he felt in his pockets for the car keys he felt a lump in his jacket pocket. He frowned and took the object out.

He almost dropped it when he saw what it was. He'd forgotten he still had it. He'd have to get rid of it at the first opportunity, he decided.

It would look bad if he was found to be carrying Sarah Hackett's wallet.

CHAPTER SIXTEEN

Judge Hackett opened the door of his flat himself. For Makepeace it was like taking a trip back in time. Suddenly she was a school girl again, standing before the tall, frightening form of Sir Lionel.

He was older now, and his face was haggard from the day's awful shock, but he seemed as stern and intimidating as she remembered him.

'Yes, what do you want?' he demanded, giving both Dempsey and her a challenging stare. Then his eyes widened slightly with surprise as he recognized her. 'Good Lord – Harriet . . .'

She smiled weakly. 'Hello, Sir Lionel. I . . . I don't know what to say. I'm just so sorry . . .'

'I know – there's no need to add anything else. It's too soon – too early . . .'

Feeling acutely uncomfortable, Makepeace indicated Dempsey. 'This is Lieutenant Dempsey. He's, er, sort of on loan to us from New York City. We work together.'

Dempsey held out his hand. 'Evening, Judge. Wish we were meeting in happier circumstances.'

Sir Lionel shook his hand, a frown on his face. 'Good evening . . .' He turned to Makepeace. 'Don't tell me you and Lieutenant Dempsey are involved in . . .'

She nodded. 'Gordon Spikings is my superior. I thought you knew.'

'No – no, I had no idea. Sarah kept me up to date with your career but she never mentioned who you worked for. No reason that she should have, of course . . .'

'Mind if we come in, Sir Lionel?' she asked gently.

'Oh, forgive me. Yes, please come in.' He stepped aside and ushered them in.

107

The flat, situated on the 20th floor of the Barbican Tower, was spacious but spartan in its furnishings. It's as austere as its owner, thought Makepeace as she entered the living room.

But the view from the wide living room window was magnificent, offering a panorama of the whole City of London. Dempsey walked over to the window and peered out. 'Hey, this is really something,' he said approvingly.

Sir Lionel regarded him quizzically. 'I must admit I still don't understand how you, an American, Lieutenant Dempsey, can be empowered to function as a police officer in this country . . .'

'Believe me, Sir Lionel,' said Makepeace quickly, 'It's all legal and above-board. It's a long and complicated story but Dempsey has special dispensation from the Home Secretary.'

'I see,' said the Judge, still looking doubtful. 'Please sit down,' he told them. 'I'd offer you a drink but of course you're both on duty . . .'

Dempsey watched with a pained expression as Sir Lionel poured himself a brandy but said nothing.

'Sir Lionel,' said Makepeace hesitantly, 'I've been meaning to call Richard . . .'

The Judge shook his head. 'I'd leave it until tomorrow. The poor boy's under sedation at the moment. I spoke to his secretary just an hour ago.'

Makepeace nodded. 'Dempsey and I are on our way down to Pangley. I may drop in on him later . . .' She took a deep breath. 'Sir Lionel, this isn't easy for me. You know how close Sarah and I were, but I must ask you to reconsider your decision about the autopsy . . .'

'The sooner the better, sir,' cut in Dempsey.

'No!' cried the Judge. 'No autopsy. I will not allow it!' He began to pace the room. 'I will not allow some nasty little butcher anywhere near my daughter. She's been abused enough.'

'But Judge,' protested Dempsey. 'You're making our

108

job a lot harder than it needs to be. An autopsy would at least tell us something about the guy who raped her. Like his blood group . . .'

Sir Lionel stopped pacing and turned to him. 'Don't presume to lecture about things I am well aware of, Lieutenant,' he said coldly. 'I've spent a whole lifetime with rapists and murderers and every other sort of criminal. I've prosecuted and judged them and I'll tell you something, young man, there's nothing you can tell me about how the Metropolitan Police work.

'An innocent young woman was raped – she put up a fight and because of her struggle she was stabbed several times with the weapon that was intended to make her submit. And then, afterwards, her throat was slit as if she was just some farm animal. There was no ulterior motive, there are no witnesses and no clues other than those that can be found by your forensic people from her clothes and from the railway compartment. But somewhere in all that revolting chain of events there is a weak link – and your job is to find it without taking any more knives to my poor daughter! Understand?'

His tirade finished Sir Lionel went and shakily poured himself another brandy. 'I'm sorry,' he added in a softer voice. 'But I'm not Joe Public. There is a difference, you know.'

Dempsey said, 'The difference is, sir, that you're using your privileged position to obstruct our investigation.'

Sir Lionel's blue eyes glittered dangerously but before he could reply Makepeace said hurriedly, 'There is one possible clue, Sir Lionel. The man I saw at the station when I dropped Sarah off. You've probably seen the photo-fit picture on TV . . .'

He shook his head. 'I don't have a TV set.'

Makepeace glanced around the room and saw this was true. She opened her briefcase and took out a copy of the picture. 'He may not have even got on the same train but he did follow Sarah into the station and he was certainly acting in an odd way . . .' She handed him the picture. He looked at it with a mixture of scorn and indifference.

'I don't suppose you recognize him, do you?' asked Makepeace. 'I thought he might be a local Pangley man . . .'

Sir Lionel shook his head. 'Never seen him before,' he said brusquely. 'And I'm sure I'd remember a face like that.'

Disappointed, Makepeace reached over to take the picture back but Sir Lionel held onto it. 'Do you have any objection if I keep this?' he asked. 'Just in case . . . ?'

'No, not at all.' She stood up. 'We must be going. If you change your mind about the autopsy . . . please call us.' She handed him a card. 'That's our number.'

He took the card but said, 'I'll not be changing my mind, Harriet.'

As they waited for the lift in the passageway outside Makepeace said to Dempsey, 'You sounded like Perry Mason in there.'

'What do you mean?'

'You telling him that he was using his privilege to obstruct our investigation.'

'Well, he is, isn't he?'

'You don't talk to a British High Court Judge that way.'

Dempsey laughed. 'You may not, princess, but where I come from that's how you talk to stubborn old ass-holes, no matter what kind of fancy title they have.'

She sighed. 'Dempsey, you're impossible.'

'Me? What about him? We're trying to find his daughter's killer and he's getting in our way. Why? That's what I'd like to know . . .'

*

110

Sir Lionel stood by the big living room window, staring with unseeing eyes out across the city. Very slowly, and very methodically, he was tearing the picture of John Bates into very small pieces.

The Panda patrol car was just emerging from a side street when Bates' Mini shot by at a speed of around fifty mph. Apart from breaking the speed limit the Mini was also travelling without any lights.

Inside the Panda Constable Driscoll sighed and said, 'Just our luck. Ten minutes before knocking-off time too.'

His companion, Constable Hulbert – who was behind the wheel – also sighed. 'Shit. And I bet he's had a few as well, which will mean another three hours at least. So much for your date with that piece from the Gas Showrooms.'

'We could always ignore it, I suppose.'

'Yeah.' But instead Hulbert swung the car out into the main road and put his foot down on the accelerator. He also switched on the Panda's flashing lights.

'She might wait, I suppose,' mused Driscoll sadly.

'Nah, no chance.'

The Duty Sergeant at the Pangley police station stopped writing as Constables Driscoll and Hulbert came into the reception area with Bates. The Sergeant, a big, jovial-faced man in his late forties who was popular with the younger officers, put down his pen and leaned on the counter. ' 'Ullo, lads. What have we got here?'

'Evening, Sarge,' said Driscoll. 'His nibs here was speeding and driving without lights.'

'Take him through,' said the Sergeant, nodding in the direction of the Charge Room.

Hulbert escorted Bates away. Driscoll remained at

the desk. 'Not very good timing, is it?' he said with a grimace.

The Sergeant looked at his watch. 'No, it's not. I hope you didn't plan to rush off anywhere tonight.'

'As it happens, Sarge, I did. Can I make a quick call?'

'Why – is he going to be a long job?'

'Well – he's a bit on the cusp, a bit iffy if you know what I mean. Going to have to get the doc in for a blood test.'

'And you've obviously got something lined up, right?' said the Sergeant, looking sympathetic.

'Yeah. All set to deflower that bird from the Gas Showrooms. I was supposed to meet her in The Three Greyhounds in a quarter of an hour. But by the time I get through here she'll have gone off the boil.'

The Sergeant said 'tsk tsk' and then asked, 'Where does matey come from?'

'He's local. Name's John Bates. Used to go to the same school as my elder brother – he's a bit . . .' Driscoll tapped his head. '. . . you know. And he's been acting funny ever since we nicked him. First he burst into tears like a baby and now he's clammed up tight. Won't say a word.'

'And you think he's been on the booze?'

'Yeah. You can smell it on his breath, Sarge.'

'But the breathalyser didn't show positive?'

'Like I said, Sarge, it was on the cusp, in my opinion. But you know what I think of these new breath test gizmos. Get better results with the old white line method . . .'

The Sergeant held up a hand. 'Yeah, so you keep saying. Okay, I'll give the doctor a call.'

Constable Driscoll looked uncomfortable. 'About *my* phone call, Sarge . . .'

'Go ahead,' he said, gesturing at the phone. 'But if you make it with this Gas Showroom bird tonight try and make sure you don't leave a bun in her oven, eh . . . ?'

The Sergeant burst out laughing at his joke. Driscoll forced a smile and a weak chuckle as he picked up the phone.

It was dark in Sir Lionel's flat. He was still standing motionless by the window, looking at the lights of the city. Then, abruptly, he turned and went into his bedroom. He switched on the light and walked quickly to a large closet set flush in the wall. He opened it and took out a double-barrelled shotgun.

CHAPTER SEVENTEEN

Spikings, his face displaying a mixture of annoyance and frustration, paced up and down his office. Chas Jarvis watched him worriedly. When Spikings was in this sort of mood life became extremely difficult.

'Okay, so how many names have we got of the people who were on that train?' he demanded.

'Two hundred and fourteen at the last count, sir,' said Jarvis.

'How many have we checked out yet?'

'They're spread around all over the Home Counties, but the response so far, particularly from the TV, has been terrific. Trouble is we'll not know how complete the passenger list is until we get the figures from British Rail, and even they won't be totally accurate.'

'Why's that?' demanded Spikings.

'Well – if some of the passengers bought tickets from a travel agent British Rail won't know until the travel agent sends in their month's return. And a proportion of the passengers may have season tickets, and we've no way of checking whether they travelled or not.'

'But surely British Rail have a record of all season ticket holders!' cried Spikings.

'Yes,' said Jarvis patiently. 'By name and address, but most of those season ticket holders travel in the rush hour, to and from work – there would be thousands of them.'

'Get them!' snapped Spikings.

'What – all of them?' Jarvis was incredulous.

'All of them.'

*

Bates stood nervously in front of the Duty Sergeant. Between them the contents of Bates' pockets were laid out on the counter.

'Right, Mr Bates,' said the Sergeant with the usual theatrical flourish he employed when dealing with members of the public. 'If you'd just like to check your belongings to make sure they're all there; handkerchief, packet of fags, matches, watch, twenty-seven pounds in notes and three pounds and sixty-four pence in loose change – sign here.' He turned the 45/7 proforma around and pointed to where Bates' signature was required.

Bates signed. His feeling of relief at having hidden Sarah Hackett's wallet – after taking out all the money – shortly before the police stopped him was so acute he was trembling.

The Sergeant peered at the signature and said, 'Thank you – here is your blood sample, sir.' He handed Bates a small, labelled bottle. 'You are at liberty to have it analysed privately – if you could just sign for that as well – here sir.'

Bates signed again.

'Thank you. I'm afraid we're going to have to keep your car in the car park here sir. Best if you come back in the morning for it.'

Bates blinked in surprise. 'Why's that?'

'Because you're still over the legal limit, sir, that's why. But these two officers will run you home.' He indicated Driscoll and Hulbert who were waiting impatiently in the background.

Bates looked at them with wide eyes. Then he said, 'Oh no, it's all right – I'll get a bus.'

The two constables laughed. The Sergeant, playing up to them, said with exaggerated surprise, 'I beg your pardon, sir?'

'I said I'll take the bus. It's no trouble – really.'

'Hark at that, Sarge,' said Driscoll. 'He says he'll take the bus.'

115

'I'm afraid we must insist, sir,' the Sergeant told Bates. He turned to Driscoll. 'Go on, get moving. If you're quick enough she may still be waiting when you get back . . .'

As the Panda car with Bates inside moved off down the street Makepeace's Jaguar pulled up in front of the police station. As Makepeace switched off the ignition Dempsey said, 'You still convinced about this guy being local?'

'I'm not convinced about anything, but it's not beyond the bounds of possibility that he was no stranger to Sarah. Statistically, over seventy per cent of rapists know their victims, and Sarah was a local girl.'

'So what does that mean?'

'Well, it means that her highest proportion of friends or acquaintances would be local as opposed to being, for example, in London. Statistically speaking, that is . . .'

'Yeah, well I don't trust statistics,' said Dempsey. 'You can use them to prove whatever you want. Me, I'd prefer to rely on a more old-fashioned device – this . . .' He tapped the side of his nose.

'Your nose?'

'The best tool a good cop can have. It never fails me.'

Makepeace sighed and said, 'Well, words fail me, Dempsey. Come on, let's go . . .'

They got out of the car and went into the station. The Sergeant gave them an enquiring look. 'Good evening – Can I help you?'

'Yeah, you can. This is Detective Sergeant Makepeace and my name's Dempsey. We're S.I.10. Working on the Hackett murder case. We got some photo-fit pictures of the suspect here for you . . .' Dempsey threw a pile of the pictures on the counter but the Sergeant

116

ignored them. Instead he stared open-mouthed at Dempsey.

Dempsey turned and said wearily to Makepeace, 'Shall I tell him or will you?'

'Lieutenant Dempsey, my partner, *is* American,' Makepeace told the Sergeant. 'Your ears do not deceive you. Unfortunately.'

'Hey, you called me "partner"!' said Dempsey delightedly.

'I used the term loosely.'

The Duty Sergeant looked from one to the other uncomprehendingly. 'You're both police officers?' he asked.

Makepeace gave him a withering look. 'Yes, *both* of us. Do you want to see some identification?'

'Uh, no . . . that won't be necessary,' he said doubtfully.

Makepeace tapped the top picture. 'The suspect – do you recognize him?'

The Sergeant stared at the photo-fit. 'Mmmm, well, I can't say as he rings any bells. It's funny how these things make everyone look like a criminal. He the only suspect?'

'Yes – well, he's not exactly a suspect even. He was seen at your railway station this morning but we don't even know for sure that he was on the same train as the Judge's daughter.'

The Sergeant shook his head and picked up the copies. 'Nasty business. I'll make sure these are circulated as soon as possible.' As he walked off he called, 'Care for a cuppa?'

'Lovely,' said Makepeace.

When the Sergeant had gone Dempsey said, 'Cuppa what?'

'Tea, of course.'

'I was afraid you'd say that.'

*

Dempsey and Makepeace were just finishing their cups of tea when Constables Driscoll and Hulbert returned. They looked questioningly at the pair of them as they entered.

'This is Detective Sergeant Makepeace and Lieutenant Dempsey,' said the Sergeant, who was just pinning up the photo-fit picture on the notice board. 'They're from S.I.10, so you two better watch your step. They're working on the Hackett case.'

The two constables looked suitably impressed, though somewhat surprised as well. Both of them seemed more interested in Makepeace than Dempsey. She smiled at them and then glanced at her watch. 'C'mon, Dempsey. We'd better get up to the railway station. The station master promised to have every single employee available for questioning, and we should have been there five minutes ago . . .'

They were just about to leave when Driscoll noticed the photo-fit and said, 'Hey, who's that?'

'The nearest thing to a suspect we've got,' said Makepeace. 'Why? Do you recognize him?'

Driscoll went to the notice board and placed his hands on each side of the face, blocking off the long hair. 'I dunno for sure . . . but it could be Bates. What do you think, Colin?'

Constable Hulbert peered at the picture over Driscoll's shoulder and said, uncomfortably, 'Pass.'

'Bates? Who's he?' asked Dempsey.

'We pulled him tonight – on a drink-drive charge,' explained Driscoll. 'We've just come back from taking him home.'

'You – took – him – home?' asked Makepeace slowly.

'It's the usual practice,' said the Sergeant.

'You think this is the same man?' asked Dempsey.

'Well, it's the hair that's different. Bates' hair is real short . . .'

'Yeah. Looked like he'd fallen into a bloody lawn-mower,' said the Sergeant.

118

'Like maybe a rush job?' asked Dempsey.

The Sergeant gave a hesitant nod. 'Yeah, well now that you mention it, I suppose . . .'

'You said you took him home,' Makepeace cut in quickly. 'Does that mean his car's still here?'

'Yessir. I mean, yes, ma'am.'

'So let's take a look,' said Dempsey.

John Bates' car sat in the police car park at the rear of the station. The security lights provided ample illumination as the Sergeant unlocked the car door for Dempsey who climbed inside and began to search the interior. After checking the obvious places, like the glove box, Dempsey reached down and felt under the driver's seat.

'Hey, what's this?' he said, producing a wallet. 'Looks kind of top drawer . . .'

He handed it to Makepeace who immediately gasped. 'It's Sarah's . . .' she whispered.

Dempsey got out of the car and gave the three uniformed officers a long, hard stare. Their shared feeling of embarrassment was obviously acute.

'So you gave him a lift home, huh?' Dempsey asked, his contempt plain.

'How were we supposed . . . ?' began the Sergeant.

'Save it. Let's go.'

Bates was just throwing clothes into an old suitcase when he heard the distinct rattle of the chain on the front door. He froze. Had the police come back? But surely the police would just bang on the door – they wouldn't try and sneak in. He strained to listen, his heart beating fast . . .

There was another sound. This time it was the sound of wood splintering as it was slowly prised apart.

Bates dropped the bundle of clothes he was holding

119

and looked anxiously around the room. Where could he hide?

There was a *snap* from downstairs. Something had given way completely. Whoever it was down there could now enter.

'Jesus,' muttered Bates. He was trembling now like a frightened rabbit. He thought about getting under the bed but dismissed the idea. Where else?

Then he noticed the wardrobe. It was the largest item of furniture in the room. As quietly as possible he went over to it, slid open one of its sliding doors and climbed inside.

There was a loud *creak* on the stairs.

Bates tried to slide the door shut but it jammed on something, leaving a gap of four inches. As hard as he pushed he couldn't close it. His eyes filled with tears.

There was another creak – this time from one of the loose floorboards in the passageway outside his room.

Frantically, Bates tried again to shut the door. Then he looked down and saw that the end of his dressing gown, which had fallen off its hanger, was jamming the door. He pulled the protruding piece of cloth inside with his foot and, at last, managed to slide the door all the way.

In the total darkness Bates listened intently. He heard footsteps outside his bedroom door and then a squeak of hinges as the door was pushed open. Then the footsteps came closer.

Bates held his breath but his heart was beating so hard he was sure it could be heard throughout the whole house.

The footsteps moved slowly around his room, pausing now and then. Then they stopped right in front of the wardrobe. Bates bit into his lower lip to stop himself from crying out.

One of the wardrobe doors was slid open. But it was the one opposite to where Bates was concealed. He heard the door being slid shut again. The tension was unbearable as he waited for his door to be opened next but to his overwhelming relief he heard the footsteps move on.

They then left the room and a short time later he heard the creak as someone went downstairs.

He let his breath out in a long, slow sigh.

He waited there in the darkness but there were no more sounds from downstairs. The intruder had obviously gone.

He slid the wardrobe door open . . . and gasped as the twin barrels of a shotgun came through the gap and nudged him in the throat.

CHAPTER EIGHTEEN

Dempsey and Makepeace pulled up in front of the Bates' house. The Panda car, which they'd followed from the station, was already parked ahead of them.

The two constables waited deferentially for the S.I.10 officers to get out and then followed them up to the front door.

'Looks like somebody used a crowbar on this,' said Dempsey, pointing at the splintered door.

They went inside. Dempsey drew his .44 Magnum – an action which produced incredulous looks from the two constables.

Warily, Dempsey checked the front room first. Mrs Bates still lay beside the TV set. He hurried over to her and hunkered down beside her, feeling her throat for a pulse.

'Is she still alive?' asked Makepeace.

'Yeah. Just. Heartbeat's very weak.'

Makepeace turned. 'Call an ambulance right away,' she ordered Driscoll. As he hurried back to the Panda she said to Hulbert, 'You stay here with the woman. Dempsey and I'll check upstairs. Whoever did this may still be up there.'

Dempsey and Makepeace proceeded as quietly as they could up the stairs, Dempsey in the lead.

Spikings looked up as his office door opened. It was Jarvis. Spikings scowled at him. 'What are you doing back here?' he asked. 'Don't you know what bloody time it is?'

Jarvis shrugged. 'Thought I might as well try and

make myself useful instead of wasting my time sleeping . . .'

'You should have stayed in bed. All I'm doing is playing silly buggers with this lot.' He gestured at the pile of computer printouts on his desk.

'What are they?'

'Lists,' sighed Spikings. 'Names and addresses categorized by post code, age, sex, profession, the lot. Big Brother is watching you, Chas. We've got Senior Citizens who have a railcard; season ticket holders; student railcard holders; British Rail employees; a hundred and twelve schoolchildren who were travelling from Reading to Slough; a football team from Bristol and a group of clergymen who were going to a religious think-in at Woking – but no John Bates.'

Jarvis frowned. 'Who is John Bates?'

'Bates is Makepeace's photo-fit. We identified him just a short time ago. He got breathalysed by one of the local Pangley Pandas . . .'

'He's in custody then?'

'Not quite. The local boys took him home. But Dempsey and Makepeace should be feeling his collar at this very moment. When they called me they were on their way to his house.'

'You think he's our man?'

'Pretty certain. He had Sarah Hackett's wallet hidden in his car.'

Jarvis whistled with surprise. Then he said, 'So why do you need those lists if Bates is the one?'

'I want proof he was on the train, that's why. And now that you're here you can put every name and address in our Section 3 system.'

Jarvis looked stricken. 'That'll take . . .'

'Alphabetically,' added Spikings.

'Alphabetically?'

'Starting with "A" . . .' He stood up and stretched. 'I'm gonna have a shave and wash-up, then I'm popping over to that all-night greasy spoon for some nosh and necessary cholesterol. I won't be long . . .'

At the doorway he paused and said, 'Oh, by the way, can you get back to British Rail and get a breakdown of absentees, sick, dead, and dying or on holiday. All we've got is what looks like their payroll list. You'll probably get a belligerent response – their systems analysts are not happy at being hauled back to their offices either – but put your foot down.'

Jarvis sighed. 'You're right. I should have stayed in bed.'

'Okay, where is he?' asked Dempsey.

Makepeace indicated the open suitcase on the bed. 'He must have heard us coming.'

'And went where? He didn't leave by the front door.'

'And no one went out the back door either,' said Constable Hulbert. 'It's locked from the inside.'

'Then he was disturbed by someone else – before we got here. By whoever broke the front door down,' said Makepeace.

'How can we be sure that Bates didn't do that himself?' asked Dempsey. 'His mother might have locked him out so he forced his way in and then hit her over the head.'

Hulbert gave an embarrassed cough and said, 'Uh, no, sir. We saw him go inside after we dropped him off. Used a key.'

'Well, that means someone else *did* get here before us,' said Dempsey. 'But who?'

'And what did they do with him?' asked Makepeace.

Suddenly Dempsey started to sniff the air. Then he went to the open wardrobe and sniffed inside.

Makepeace turned to Constable Hulbert, who was watching Dempsey with a mystified expression, and said, 'You're seeing Lieutenant Dempsey's famous crime-fighting tool in action – his nose. After a single sniff of the suspect's clothing he will track him down to wherever he is . . .'

Dempsey withdrew his head from the wardrobe. 'What my nose *has* found is a pool of piss in the wardrobe.'

'What?' cried Makepeace. She went and looked inside. 'Ugh, you're right! Why on earth would anyone want to go and . . .'

'It probably wasn't deliberate,' said Dempsey. 'The way I see it Bates was hiding in there and someone gave him a nasty fright. He pissed his pants.'

'It must have been some fright.'

'Yeah. And I'm beginning to have a strong hunch about who gave it to him.'

Dempsey and Makepeace looked very tired as they entered Spikings' office. Spikings looked even more weary.

'Sit down before you collapse,' he told them.

They did so, thankfully. 'Still no word on Bates?' asked Makepeace.

'Nope. The whole Thames Valley Police Force are on the lookout for him but so far they've come up empty-handed. He's gone to ground – and with a vengeance.'

Dempsey and Makepeace exchanged a glance. Spikings noticed it. 'Okay, what have you got that you aren't telling me?' he demanded.

'Dempsey has a theory – and that's *all* it is,' said Makepeace.

'Well, what is it?'

Dempsey cleared his throat. 'Well, the way it looks is that someone busted into Bates' place and nabbed him.'

'So you said on the radio. I'm not sure I buy it. It could be a ploy to put us on the wrong track.'

'I don't think so, sir,' said Dempsey. 'From what one of the local cops told me about Bates he isn't smart enough to do anything like that.'

'So what's your theory?' asked Spikings.

Dempsey took a deep breath and said, 'I think the Judge got to him.'

'The Judge?' repeated Spikings blankly.

'Yeah. You know. Sir Lionel . . .'

Spikings' eyes bulged. 'Are you making some kind of weird American joke?'

'I'm serious, sir,' said Dempsey.

'I'm afraid he is,' confirmed Makepeace.

'You're crazy!' exploded Spikings. 'You're talking about Sir Lionel Hackett! A High Court judge! *The* High Court judge! The laws of this land are sacred to him! It's madness to suggest he would try and take the law into his own hands no matter what the provocation.'

'I'm sorry, sir,' persisted Dempsey. 'But that's what I *am* suggesting. I think he recognized Bates when Harry showed him the photo-fit but didn't tell us. Then he went and got him. If I was you I'd put out an APB for him as well as Bates.'

'And I'm telling you it's ridiculous!' cried Spikings. 'For God's sake, I know the man! He used to be my commanding officer in the army! He even saved my life! And you're asking me to have him arrested!' Spikings shook his head violently. 'No way. I'll forget we had this conversation, Dempsey. And now I suggest you two knock off for awhile and have a rest . . . you obviously need it.'

'But . . .' began Dempsey, but Makepeace reached over and touched him on the arm. 'The Chief is right. Let's go.' She got up. Dempsey, after a pause, did likewise. 'Okay,' he said to Spikings. 'Have it your way. I just hope you won't be sorry . . .'

*

126

They walked slowly into their office. As Makepeace collapsed into her chair Dempsey said, 'Want a coffee?'

'Please. With lots of sugar. I need the energy.'

Dempsey went off to the coffee machine. When he returned Makepeace gratefully took the plastic cup from him and said, 'Thanks. Look, do you really think that Sir Lionel has kidnapped Bates?'

'Yeah, I do. And so would you if you weren't dazzled by the fact that the guy's a judge and a "sir" and all that other British class crap.'

'Oh, Dempsey . . .' she scoffed.

'It's true. The Chief's got the same problem. No way is it possible that his upper-class ex-commanding officer could deliberately break the law. It's pathetic. The Chief practically goes down on one knee at the mention of the Judge's name . . .'

Makepeace stirred her coffee thoughtfully. 'Let's say, just for the sake of argument, that you're right – that Sir Lionel has got Bates. What do you think he'll do to him?'

'Kill him, of course. If he hasn't already . . .'

'Well, it would save the taxpayers thousands of pounds – but it wouldn't do Sir Lionel's career much good.'

'It wouldn't do Bates' career much good either – particularly if he wasn't the right guy.'

'But he *is* the right one!' said Makepeace firmly. 'I'd put a month's salary on it. Look, he knew her, he was at the station and saw her arrive. It all fits! And the ticket clerk remembers selling him a ticket after Sarah . . .'

'Okay, he bought a ticket – he could have gotten a later train.'

'Unlikely – and what about her wallet in his car? If that's not a damning piece of evidence I don't know what is.'

'It's circumstantial, like the rest of the evidence. She

127

could have dropped it somewhere in the station and he picked it up and kept it.'

'Oh, really! You can't be serious.'

He shrugged. 'You asked for my opinion and I gave it to you.'

'You gave me a load of codswallop. Which is a British term for bullshit.'

'Well, I still say you haven't any real proof that Bates raped and murdered the Judge's daughter. And without any witnesses there's only one other way of getting that proof, if it exists.'

Makepeace sipped at her coffee and said, 'And what way is that, Sherlock?'

'Autopsy. Or at least a partial autopsy . . .'

'Autopsy? But, Dempsey, that's been squashed not only by the Coroner but by the Chief Constable too!'

'I know, but it's the only way of establishing the blood type of the rapist and seeing if it matches with that of Bates.'

She looked puzzled. 'How could you get this blood type from . . .?' she began, then realization dawned. 'Oh, of course,' she muttered.

'You handled any rape cases before?'

'No,' she admitted.

'Well, I had my fair share of them in New York so I know a bit about the medical procedure. And one thing I do know is we got to hurry if we're gonna prove anything . . .'

'What do you mean?'

'Well, to put it bluntly, Harry, semen breaks down pretty quickly in the female sexual organs – even in dead bodies. If we wait much longer there won't be anything left to analyse . . .'

Makepeace winced.

'Hey, I'm sorry, princess. I know she was a friend of yours but it has to be done . . .'

'Dempsey,' said Makepeace impatiently. 'Don't you understand yet? An autopsy is out of the question.'

128

'Yeah. Sure. Now, what's the name of that Jamaican doctor who you busted a couple of weeks back for supplying hard drugs to his junkie friends?'

'Roberts. And he's not a Jamaican – he's from Bermuda. Why? What's that got to do with anything?'

'Can you get to him?'

She sighed. 'Yes – he's on bail. Are you going to tell me what you're talking about or do we just keep on playing this game?'

'What I'm talking about, princess, is a break-in.'

'A break-in?'

'Yeah. We're going to break into the morgue.'

CHAPTER NINETEEN

Sir Lionel Hackett was walking in a rather furtive manner along a path besides the Thames that led to a boathouse. Even in the darkness the boathouse was obviously in a dilapidated condition.

At the entrance to the building he paused and looked around him but there was nothing to see but the trees, their branches moving slightly in the stiff night breeze. There were no houses nearby and he felt confident no one would hear the sounds of his work.

He went inside, switched on the powerful flashlight he'd been carrying and placed it on a bench so that it cast its light over the widest possible area. Also on the bench were a number of carpentry tools that he'd put there earlier.

He picked up a piece of chalk and a ruler, bent down and marked out a three foot wide square on the loose floorboards of the boathouse. Then he got a saw, put the blade between one of the wide gaps between the planks and began to saw.

There was a smile on his face as he worked.

Dempsey leaned on Dr Roberts' front door and muttered, 'I hope to hell he hasn't skipped bail.'

'I hope to hell he has,' said Makepeace glumly.

They were standing in the first floor corridor of a fairly expensive block of mansion flats in the Fulham Road. The time was now nearly 3 am.

The door finally opened. Dr Roberts was a small, dapper-looking black man in his early forties. He was wearing a silk dressing gown and had a 9 mm Browning pistol in his manicured hand.

Dempsey glanced down at the gun and said, 'Tsk, tsk . . .'

'What do you want? Who are you?' demanded Dr Roberts. Then he recognized Makepeace and his face fell. 'Sergeant Makepeace . . . Oh, goodness . . .'

'You can say that again, sweetheart,' growled Dempsey. He plucked the gun from Roberts' hand and examined it. 'You get this on the National Health Service?'

'Look, I can explain that. I need protection. I have many enemies . . .'

'I can understand why.'

Roberts looked pleadingly at Makepeace. 'Who *is* this man?' he asked her.

'My partner,' said Makepeace wearily. 'We've come to ask you a favour . . .'

'Yeah,' said Dempsey. 'A favour.' He put his hand on Roberts' chest and propelled him backwards into his flat. 'First we ask the favour nicely then we do it the hard way.'

As Makepeace closed the door of the flat, Dempsey kept pushing Roberts backwards across his living room until he was forced to sit down heavily on a sofa. He stared up at Dempsey in dismay. 'Have you got a warrant?' he cried.

'You got a permit for that gun?'

Roberts' shoulders sagged even further.

'You're already in big trouble, Dr Roberts,' Makepeace told him. 'Now you're in even bigger trouble.'

Roberts said nothing.

Dempsey looked around the living room. 'Nice place you got here. All the latest mod-cons and gadgets. Big TV, video, hi-fi . . . you're going to miss all this when they put you away next month.'

'I want to call my solicitor,' said Roberts in a dead voice.

'I don't think he'd appreciate you waking him up at this time of the night, no matter how much you pay

131

him,' said Dempsey. 'But before you open your wrists we have a little proposition for you that might make you feel better.'

'What is it?' he asked suspiciously.

'We need your help. Your medical help. Right now. You play ball and Sergeant Makepeace here will use her influence with the court to make things easier for you when your case comes up.'

Roberts looked at Makepeace. There was a tiny flicker of hope in his eyes. 'Is this true?'

Makepeace nodded reluctantly.

'What do you want me to do then?'

Dempsey told him.

When Dempsey had finished Dr Roberts said softly, 'Oh, goodness . . .'

The last section of plank fell into the river with a splash. The Judge stood up, sweating heavily. There was now a ragged square cut in the floor of the boathouse. The dark, swiftly moving water of the river could be seen beneath it.

The Judge gazed down at his work with satisfaction and then looked at John Bates.

Bates was trussed up like a chicken and propped against one of the boathouse walls. A rope around his neck was tied to a metal mooring ring.

There was a gag in his mouth. His eyes, as they followed the Judge's every move, bulged with terror.

'I must need my head examined,' muttered Makepeace as she climbed out of her car.

'Your pal the doc would probably do it for free,' said Dempsey. 'But first he's got a more pressing appointment. Right, doc?'

Dr Roberts, now dressed, incongruously, in the leather jacket and trousers of a motor cyclist, nodded within the confines of the over-sized crash helmet he was wearing.

They were parked in front of the Police Morgue in Horseferry Road. It was now a quarter to four and there was a chill in the air. Makepeace shivered and looked up and down the deserted street. 'At least we won't have far to go when we're arrested. Scotland Yard's just round the corner . . .'

'Hey, cut the negative thoughts,' said Dempsey, giving her shoulder a reassuring squeeze. 'This is gonna be a piece of cake. You know what to do?'

'Yes,' she muttered.

'Then let's go.'

The three of them entered the building, Dempsey and Makepeace flanking Roberts. The police constable on duty at the reception desk looked up with a frown. He was reading a copy of *Playboy*.

Makepeace went into action. 'Morning, officer! I'm Makepeace . . .' She flashed her I.D. at him, giving him long enough to register the fact that she was a member of the elite S.I.10 unit. '. . . And this is Dempsey. We've come to carry out the formal identification of James Desmond, the hit-and-run victim. He came in this afternoon. This is his neighbour, Mr Roberts . . .' She pointed at the doctor. 'It's taken us all this time to track him down.'

The constable, having hastily put the magazine away, made a stab at brisk efficiency. 'Uh, yes, right . . . er, have you got the I.D. 48 made out?'

Makepeace turned to Dempsey. 'Have you?'

He frowned. 'Is that the green form? Or the blue one?'

'Green,' said the officer, looking at Dempsey with a puzzled expression.

'Lieutenant Dempsey's on attachment from the New York Police Department,' explained Makepeace. 'And I'm afraid he's not yet quite up to muster on our paperwork.'

'That's all right,' said the constable, though a little doubtfully. 'We've got some here.' He opened a drawer and produced a green sheet of paper. 'If you'd just like to complete that, Mr Roberts, just the name and address, your profession and so on . . .'

While Roberts filled in the form the constable pressed a button on his intercom. 'I'll get the night attendant to take you through,' he said.

A short time later the swing doors opened and a bored-looking young man dressed in white appeared. When he saw Makepeace some of his evident apathy immediately vanished. 'Hullo, what's this then?' he said in a thick East End accent, staring straight at Makepeace and ignoring the two men.

'A police officer, Ron,' said the constable quickly. 'From S.I.10. So's the gentleman. They've brought Mr Roberts here to view the hit-and-run. Take them through, will you?'

'Sure,' said the attendant and beckoned for them to follow him, his eyes still on Makepeace.

He led them through two pairs of green-painted swinging doors and into a large room that smelt strongly of disinfectant and other things that Makepeace preferred not to dwell upon.

There were two stainless-steel-topped dissection tables in the centre of the room, their surfaces glittering in the harsh light. Along one wall were the cold storage compartments, each of them neatly labelled.

Makepeace suppressed a shudder at the thought of Sarah's body lying behind one of those metal panels. Sarah – who only that morning had been a living, breathing and warm human being. Poor clumsy, awkward Sarah . . .

'You must have the Hackett girl here as well,' said Dempsey loudly, brutally cutting into her thoughts. 'A couple of our colleagues are working on that case.'

'Yeah,' said the attendant. 'She's in number six. Someone really did a job on her. The bastards . . .'

He grabbed the large handle on one of the compartment doors and pulled. The coffin-sized metal drawer slid out from the wall with a squeak of badly oiled rollers. Inside lay a figure covered with a green sheet.

The attendant took hold of the sheet then hesitated. 'I gotta warn you he's not a pretty sight, know what I mean? The van that hit him dragged him along the road for about fifty yards . . .'

'Go ahead,' ordered Dempsey.

The sheet was pulled back from what was left of James Desmond's face.

Makepeace made a small 'Oh' sound and then slumped to the floor.

Dempsey looked down at her dispassionately and said to the attendant, 'Oh God – it's times like these I wonder if women are really viable as cops.' He shook his head. 'Can you manage to get her into some fresh air? I'll finish off here with Mr Roberts . . .'

The attendant said eagerly, 'Yeah, be happy to!'

Dempsey helped the young man get Makepeace to her feet and then watched as he half-dragged and half-carried her away, noting with amusement that he was being deliberately careless about where he was putting his hands. Makepeace was no doubt furious but could do nothing about it.

When the two of them had disappeared through the first set of swing doors Dempsey turned to Roberts and said urgently, 'Quick . . . number six.'

Together they pulled out the drawer then removed the sheet from Sarah Hackett. Dempsey winced at the ragged knife wounds on her body. Worst of all was the wound across her throat. It gaped open like the gill of a fish.

'Help me carry her to one of the tables!' said Roberts. 'I need room to work . . .'

Reluctantly Dempsey put his hands under her shoulders and lifted. Her flesh was cold and rubbery to the touch and he suddenly felt nauseous. The strong odour

135

of formaldehyde didn't help. Struggling, they got her out of the compartment and over to one of the dissection tables. She was only slimly built but like all dead bodies she seemed unnaturally heavy. Dempsey tried to avoid looking at her eyes which were half-open.

When they'd laid her out on the metal table Roberts hurriedly removed his shoulder bag and produced a scalpel, and three clear plastic bags. One of the bags contained rubber gloves, one was full of cotton swabs, the other was empty.

Dempsey eyed the scalpel with alarm as Roberts pulled on the gloves. 'What's the knife for?'

'What do you think?' snapped Roberts, plainly very nervous and agitated. 'I don't have the time to do the job correctly – I'm just going to cut everything out and take it away with me. The detailed examination will have to wait until later. Understand?'

'Yeah . . .' said Dempsey, his mouth dry.

He watched as the doctor got to work. But when Roberts made the first incision Dempsey switched his attention to the swing doors, trying to block his ears to the sounds as well. He hated autopsies.

'How did I get into this mess?' moaned Roberts as he worked.

'That's probably what *she'd* like to know, wherever she is,' said Dempsey. 'And that's what we're here to find out.'

The long seconds dragged by. Dempsey expected to see the attendant come back through the swinging doors at any moment. If he did it was going to be a very embarrassing situation for all concerned.

But then, less than two minutes after he'd begun, Roberts said hoarsely, 'I've finished . . . hurry, we must get her back into the compartment . . .'

Averting his eyes from the doctor's handiwork Dempsey helped him carry the body over to the drawer. While Dempsey slid the compartment shut Roberts hurried back to the table and began to sluice the blood away, then peeled off his gloves and put them back into one of the plastic bags.

'Well, we did it...' began Dempsey but then he noticed Roberts' eyes widening with alarm. He was staring at something on the floor – behind Dempsey.

Dempsey turned and saw that the sheet that had been covering Sarah Hackett was lying there. They'd both forgotten it...

'Oh, shit,' said Dempsey. He rushed back to it, snatched it up, hauled open the drawer again and tossed it in. He was just about to push the compartment shut when he heard a voice cry, ' 'Ere, what the hell are you up to?'

CHAPTER TWENTY

Dempsey calmly slid the drawer shut and turned. The attendant stood in the doorway looking annoyed.

'Just wanted to have a glance at the Hackett girl while I was here,' said Dempsey as casually as possible. He was relieved to see that Roberts had put away the three incriminating plastic bags. And the steel-topped table was once again spotless. There was no visible sign of what they'd been up to. 'Like you said, some bastard really did a job on her...' He gestured to Roberts. 'Come on, sir, we can go now.'

The two of them walked past the attendant and back to the reception area.

As they got in the car Makepeace said anxiously. 'Well? Don't keep me in suspense...'

'We made it. *Just*,' Dempsey told her. 'If that morgue guy had returned a few seconds earlier it would have been curtains.'

'I did my best to keep him occupied, the randy little creep,' she said. 'But when you took so long in there he started to get worried. You must have activated a long dormant sense of duty within him...'

'Hey, you did all right, princess,' he assured her. 'You'd make a great actress.'

'That's good to know – that I have something to fall back on when my career in the police force comes to a premature end, which it is sure to do at any moment now.'

'I want to go home. I don't feel well,' said Dr Roberts who was sitting in the back seat with his face buried in his hands.

Dempsey said, 'I know how you feel, doc. I'm kind of queasy myself . . .'

'You don't understand. I need a fix.'

'Well, you're going to have to wait. We got to get those specimens in your bag checked out.'

'But my lab assistant friend is off-duty and the hospital is shut for the night,' Roberts whined.

'You know where your friend lives, don't you?'

'Yes, of course. In Battersea.'

'Good. Just a few minutes' drive away,' said Dempsey cheerfully. 'We go pick him up and take him to the hospital. He'll have the keys to the lab, won't he?'

'I suppose so . . .' muttered Roberts.

'Dempsey, what are you suggesting?' asked Makepeace.

'If we can get into a police lab, perform a partial autopsy on a body and get out again, then breaking into a hospital should be like taking a bed bath from a beautiful nurse.'

'Oh no,' sighed Makepeace. She turned and looked out the window.

'I don't want to have any more to do with this,' said Roberts. 'I insist you take me home.'

Dempsey leaned over the back of the seat and grinned at Roberts. 'Doc, you're going to quit your whining and do as I say or I'm going to give you a lead enema. Savvy?'

Roberts swallowed and nodded.

'Good. Now give me the directions to your friend's place. We're running out of time.'

'So far so good,' said Dempsey with satisfaction.

Makepeace gave a hollow laugh. 'So far so *good*? My career, such as it was, is now in tatters. I am about to die through lack of sleep. I'm afraid to go back to my flat because undoubtedly Spikings – my ex-boss by now – has got the place staked out as we are both probably on the Wanted List. If that's *good* you must be using an American definition of the word.'

'Have another cup of coffee. You'll feel better.'

'No, thank you. My cells are saturated with caffeine as it is. Any more and I'll unravel across the floor.'

They were sitting together on two lab stools and leaning wearily on a counter. The lab itself – located in the basement of a small, exclusive private hospital in Hampstead – was filled with all the latest and most expensive equipment.

Roberts and his friend – who, surprisingly, had turned out to be a strikingly attractive young girl – were still hard at work with their analysis of the smears taken from the specimens that Roberts had acquired. It was now almost 6 am and the sky was starting to lighten.

Roberts was hunched over a computer. He looked healthier than he had earlier and Dempsey suspected he'd managed to give himself a surreptitious injection, but he was in no position to complain.

At that moment the doctor tore off a printout from the computer and conferred with his friend. She nodded her head and Roberts turned to Dempsey and Makepeace.

'Well,' he said, 'we've got two results which may be significant . . .'

'So give,' ordered Dempsey.

'The first is that either the victim or the rapist had syphilis.'

'Can't you tell which?' asked Dempsey.

'Not at this stage. All that we can tell is that the disease is present.'

'It couldn't be Sarah,' said Makepeace. 'She was a virgin. I know that for certain.'

Roberts looked surprised. 'A virgin? At her age?'

Makepeace glowered at him. 'Yes. Incredible, isn't it?'

140

'So it has to be the guy with the dose, right?' Dempsey asked Roberts quickly.

'Obviously,' said Roberts.

'That means if Bates has got syphilis we've got definite proof he's our man.'

'Yes,' agreed Roberts.

'What's the second result?'

'Well, the second one is a little more specific than the first. We did an electro-phonesis test on the semen smears and established that the rapist had a Pep A21 blood type.'

'Gee, I'm real impressed,' said Dempsey with heavy sarcasm. 'Now would you mind explaining to me what the fuck that means?'

'It means that the rapist was black.'

Dempsey said, 'Huh?'

'The rapist – and murderer – was black,' repeated Roberts. 'I presume John Bates is black?'

Dempsey and Makepeace exchanged a glance. 'No,' said Dempsey.

'Then you've got the wrong man,' said Roberts, shrugging.

'*Someone*'s got the wrong man,' muttered Dempsey.

Spikings was still poring over his computer printouts when Dempsey and Makepeace burst into his office. 'Where the hell have you been? Chas has been trying to raise you two for hours!'

'Sorry, Chief, but we've been following up some leads on our own bat,' said Makepeace. 'Have they picked up Bates yet?'

'No. No bleeding sign of the sod . . . What do you *mean* you've been following up leads on your own?'

'We'll explain later, sir,' said Dempsey. 'The important thing is that Bates isn't our pigeon. The rapist was a black.'

Spikings stared at him. 'You what?'

141

'It's true,' said Makepeace. 'Bates isn't the one. I was wrong. And if you promise to listen without losing your temper I'll explain how we know.'

'I don't like the sound of *that*. What have you been up to?'

Makepeace told him. He was silent when she finished. Finally he said, very quietly, 'If any of this comes out in court you're both on your own.'

'We knew we could count on your support, sir,' said Dempsey dryly.

Spikings glared at him. 'What do you expect? You enter a police morgue under false pretences and help a junkie slice up the body of a High Court judge's daughter?'

'Extenuating circumstances, sir,' said Makepeace. 'We had no choice if we wanted to establish the truth about John Bates . . .'

'Which we *have* done,' said Dempsey. 'Which means your friend the Judge has gone after the wrong man.'

Spikings groaned. 'You're still not on that crazy kick, are you?'

'Yeah, I am. Why don't you give the Judge a call?' Dempsey nodded towards the phone. 'I'll give you ten-to-one he won't be at home.'

'I'm not calling Sir Lionel at this hour of the morning just because you have some ridiculous theory about him!'

'*I'll* call him,' said Dempsey.

'No you won't, and that's an order!'

Dempsey shrugged. 'You're going to be awful sorry about this.'

'That's my lookout. Yours is to do as I say.'

Makepeace said, 'Chief, I know it does sound ridiculous but I think Dempsey might be right about Sir Lionel.'

'You're right. It *does* sound ridiculous,' snapped Spikings. 'I don't want to hear any more of it. Our job is to track down the black who killed Sarah Hackett. Any ideas on how we're going to do it?'

Makepeace nodded. 'Only about one in four blacks have this particular blood grouping . . .' She glanced at the piece of paper that Roberts had given her. '. . . Pep A21. Plus the fact that the syphilis he's suffering from is a fairly rare type. It's an Asian variety and particularly virulent. Roberts, our tame doctor, thinks that the man must be undergoing some form of treatment for it. Which means . . .'

'Which means all we have to do is check all the VD clinics and see if any of their patients fit the bill,' said Spikings eagerly. He buzzed Jarvis.

Jarvis hurried in from the adjoining office. He looked harassed. 'I've just finished getting all those names into the system, sir. Alphabetically, as you wanted . . .'

Spikings waved a dismissive hand. 'Forget all that rubbish, Chas. We've got a new angle to follow up.'

'*Forget it?* But do you know how long . . .?'

'Shut up and listen,' growled Spikings, and then told Jarvis what Dempsey and Makepeace had discovered. 'So get moving, Chas. Harry, give him that report . . .'

As Makepeace handed him the paper she said, 'Also, Chas, could you be a dear and send someone out for a bite to eat? Dempsey and I haven't eaten for over twelve hours. I'm so hungry I could eat a hamburger.'

It was a bizarre scene. Sir Lionel Hackett was squatting down beside a tailor's dummy that lay on the floor of the boathouse next to the open square in the floorboards. Sir Lionel was carefully cutting round the outline of John Bates' face on the photo-fit picture.

When he'd finished he pasted the face onto the blank head of the dummy. Then he turned and smiled at John Bates. 'Almost ready to begin,' he told him.

CHAPTER TWENTY-ONE

'We should make a habit out of having breakfast together, princess.'

Makepeace looked at him over the top of her half-eaten hamburger, which continued to drip grease onto her desk despite all her efforts, and said, 'God, what a horrible thought.' Then she looked at the hamburger and grimaced. 'When I told Chas I could eat one of these I didn't intend for him to take me literally.'

'It doesn't always have to be hamburgers. I make a mean plate of scrambled eggs.'

'I'm sure your scrambled eggs are incredibly mean, Dempsey, but I think I'd prefer the scrambled eggs at Claridge's.'

He frowned. 'Who's he? A boyfriend?'

'Oh, Dempsey . . .' She finished the hamburger and then took a pile of tissues out of her handbag, along with a mirror and comb. After meticulously cleaning her hands she looked in the mirror. 'I look awful.'

'You look okay to me.'

'Those are just your glands speaking, Dempsey, so I won't pay any attention.' She started to comb her hair. Just then the intercom buzzed. It was Jarvis. Spikings wanted them in the computer room immediately.

'We got a candidate!' cried Spikings as they entered. He was standing behind Jarvis who was at work on the computer keyboard. 'Name is William Thornton. Aged twenty-eight. Found him on the files of a VD clinic attached to Paddington General Hospital. And get this – our boy has form. Show them, Chas . . .'

Dempsey and Makepeace saw the details of Thornton's criminal record appear on the display screen.

Two convictions of Assault with GBH. Served six months in Wormwood Scrubs for the first conviction and a year for the second.

'Got an address for him?' asked Dempsey.

Jarvis nodded, touching the keyboard again. 'Seventeen Westbrook Square, Ladbroke Grove.'

'So what was he doing on the train from Pangley if he lives in London?' asked Makepeace.

'I don't suppose, by any chance, that the judge who sent him down was Hackett?' asked Dempsey.

Jarvis checked, then shook his head. 'Nope. Sorry.'

'There goes that theory,' said Dempsey. 'No motive so it must have been a spur-of-the-moment attack.'

'Want to go ask Mr Thornton personally about that?' said Spikings. 'Or shall I send someone else? You two look pretty beat.'

Dempsey glanced at Makepeace. 'Shall we?'

'Let's see this thing through to the bitter end,' she said grimly. 'I owe it to Sarah.'

The fully dressed tailor's dummy, with the reproduction of John Bates' face pasted to its head, was standing on the chair – held upright by the rope around its neck. The rope was looped several times around a roof beam and its end tied to a mooring ring. The chair was right on the edge of the square cut into the floor. Another piece of rope was tied to a leg of the chair. Its other end was held by Sir Lionel.

He sat in a chair about ten feet away. He was wearing his black gown and wig. The shotgun lay on his lap.

John Bates regarded him fearfully. He was still trussed up against the wall but the gag had been removed from his mouth. His face was the colour of a dirty white sheet.

'You have heard the evidence against the accused – have you reached your verdict?' Sir Lionel asked him in the sepulchral tones of a judge in his courtroom.

'You're bloody mad! That's what you are!' cried Bates in a strangled voice.

Sir Lionel lifted the shotgun and pointed it at him. 'What is your verdict? Guilty or not guilty? Did John Bates rape and murder Sarah Hackett? Did John Bates murder his mother, Mrs Joan Bates, later that same day?'

Bates stared at the muzzle of the gun, then his face crumpled. He began to whimper like a child. Tears ran down his cheeks. 'Yeah . . . I killed Mum . . . I didn't mean to . . . it was an accident . . .'

'*Silence!*' Sir Lionel's voice was like the crack of a whip. 'You admit you killed Mrs Bates. Now admit you killed Sarah Hackett!'

'I don't know . . .' he whimpered. 'I don't know any more . . .'

'Guilty or not guilty!' repeated Sir Lionel.

Bates looked at him through his tears and then, resignedly, said, 'He's guilty, m'Lord . . .'

'Very well. I shall now pronounce sentence . . .' He jerked hard on the end of the rope. The chair toppled over with a bang. The dummy was sent swinging out over the hole in the floor. The noose around its neck tightened as the rope went taut.

The dummy began to twist slowly back and forth, the rope creaking against the roof beam.

Bates stared with horror at his own face on the dummy as it turned back and forth.

Sir Lionel looked at his watch. 'Soon it will be exactly twenty-four hours since you raped and murdered my daughter. When that time arrives *you* will take the dummy's place on the chair.'

It was exactly 9.30 am when Dempsey and Makepeace parked their car in Westbrook Square. The square, just off Ladbroke Grove near the Westway flyover, was small and very dirty. 'Now I know where all the

146

garbage trucks empty their loads,' Dempsey said as he got out.

'There's the place, and it looks like we're in luck.' She pointed at number seven. From the outside the run-down house had the appearance of a squat that had seen better days but there was a loud throb of reggae coming from the open windows. 'Someone is home . . .'

'Might not be Thornton though,' said Dempsey as they negotiated their way past the split black plastic bags full of garbage.

Makepeace rang the doorbell. There was no response so she knocked hard on the door. About ten seconds later it opened a few inches and they saw a single, suspicious eye peer out at them. 'Mr Thornton?'

'Who the fuck are you? What you want?'

Makepeace summoned up her most dazzling and radiant smile. 'Good morning, sir. We're from the local council and we'd like to discuss your rent rebate.'

'Say *what*?'

'Your rent rebate, sir. As a result of a recent Rents Tribunal decision the tenants in this square are all due a large rent refund. You *are* Mr Thornton, aren't you?'

There was a flash of white teeth in the darkness and then the door was flung open. A tall, well-built black man, wearing nothing but a short bathrobe, stood there with a wide grin on his face. 'I am he! Come on in and tell me more!'

Makepeace, followed closely by Dempsey, entered the house. But just as she went through the doorway Thornton suddenly put an arm around her neck and pulled her violently to one side. At the same time there was a distinct *click* and the next thing she knew Thornton was holding a switchblade to her throat . . .

Dempsey, by this time, had drawn his .44 but it was too late. There was nothing he could do. He froze, the gun wavering in his hand.

'Drop it, you mother, or I give this doll here an extra pussy!' cried Thornton.

Dempsey dropped the gun. There was a look of self-disgust on his face.

'It's okay, Dempsey,' said Makepeace, with difficulty. 'We're both tired. It made us careless . . .'

'Shut up, bitch!' ordered Thornton, pricking her throat with the flick-knife. 'You, man! Shut the door then move over against that wall . . . hurry! Or she gonna start spurting blood farther than you can piss!'

Dempsey did as he was told.

'Shee-it!' spat Thornton, his voice high with a mixture of nervous excitement and anger. 'You think I'm some kind of stupid nigger? You think I'm gonna fall for that crap? You two got "cop" written all over you in big blue letters. Rent rebate my black ass!'

At that moment there was a movement in the doorway leading into the passageway. A tall black girl, completely naked, appeared – her eyes wide with alarm. 'Billy!' she cried. 'Wha's goin' on?'

'Get back in the bedroom, gal!' ordered Thornton. 'Stay there 'til I say otherwise.'

The girl hesitated then went.

'Okay,' said Thornton. 'The guy was carrying a piece so that means you probably is too, baby. Hey?'

'No. I'm not,' said Makepeace.

'Yeah? Well, let's take a look-see . . .' He removed his arm from around her neck but kept the blade pressed against her throat. 'Raise your arms!' he ordered.

She felt his hand run up her left side to her armpit. Then he felt her right side and patted the small of her back.

'So, you're clean,' he said, surprised. 'Okay, now we move over to that cannon your pal dropped . . . but nice and easy . . .'

Very slowly Makepeace walked to where the Magnum lay on the floor and stopped. Thornton took the knife from her throat and then dug its point into her lower back on her left side. She gasped as the knife pricked her skin.

'Stay still or you're dead meat,' warned Thornton as he bent down and picked up Dempsey's gun.

Makepeace began to sway slightly. 'I think I'm going to faint,' she moaned.

Then, abruptly, she slumped forward and landed facedown on the floor with a loud thud.

'Hey!' cried Thornton in alarm. 'Get up, bitch!' He kicked her very hard in the ribs but she lay there unmoving.

Dempsey took a step towards Thornton but the black man cocked the .44. 'Stay right there, honky, or you gonna be the new wallpaper . . .' He started to back away from Makepeace, the gun on Dempsey.

Makepeace, trying to ignore the agony that blazed through her right side, listened to the sound of Thornton's footsteps, picturing in her mind's eye his exact position and distance from her.

She had deliberately fallen on her right arm, pinning it beneath her chest. Now she began to move her hand . . .

Within seconds her right hand had closed on the butt of the small .25 Beretta concealed in the special holster between her breasts.

She twisted her body round on the floor in one sudden, galvanic movement. There was a sharp *crack* from the small gun in her hand . . .

Thornton screamed. The Magnum flew from his grip as he staggered back a step. Then he began to double over, clutching at his groin with both hands. Blood ran freely from between his fingers. He sagged down onto his knees, his scream one long continuous sound, like the screech of a siren.

Dazed, Makepeace felt herself being lifted up by a pair of strong arms. 'You okay, princess?' asked Dempsey in her ear.

'I think so,' she said shakily. 'Thanks.'

'Thank *you*. That was real nice shooting. There's gonna be a big demand for him in the prison choir – in the soprano section.'

'I didn't *deliberately* shoot him there,' she protested.

'Must have been a Freudian slip then . . . *look out!*'

Makepeace was shoved to one side. She turned to see the tall, naked black girl come rushing at them, a kitchen carving knife held high. Dempsey leapt forward and as she lunged at him with the knife he blocked her arm with his left wrist and then hit her hard on the point of her chin with his right fist. Her head snapped back and she dropped to the floor.

Dempsey looked down at her, massaging the knuckles of his right hand. 'There's got to be an easier way of making a living,' he said.

Makepeace turned to Thornton who was still on his knees clutching at his groin. His scream had died down to a kind of stomach-churning wail of agony but there was now a sizeable pool of blood on the floor beneath him.

'I'd better go call an ambulance,' she told Dempsey. 'And call the local lads round here as well . . .'

'Okay,' said Dempsey, picking up his .44. 'I'll keep these two funsters company . . . I'd put a tourniquet on this guy's problem if you'd left anything to tie up . . .'

'Humph,' she grunted.

She went outside, blinking in the sunlight. It seemed a hundred years ago since she'd been in this tawdry, dirty square yet it had only been a matter of minutes. She felt dizzy and ill and when she reached the car she leaned against it for a short time. Then she took a deep breath, winced at the pain in her ribs, and opened the car door.

After calling the emergency services she contacted Jarvis at S.I.10 and told him what had happened. Then, when she'd finished, she said, 'You can tell our beloved Commander that Dempsey and I are now going to bed – *separately* – for at least a week. No, make that a month.'

'But he's not here, Sergeant!' said Jarvis. 'He left for Pangley just a few moments ago!'

'What for?'

'Well, he started having second thoughts about what Lieutenant Dempsey said about Sir Lionel. So this morning he called the Judge's flat. He spoke to his housekeeper. She said Sir Lionel's bed hadn't been slept in. So then the Chief called Sir Lionel's house at Pangley. The Judge isn't there either. *Then* the London housekeeper calls and says she's done a check of the flat and found Sir Lionel's shotgun missing. After that the Chief took off like a damn rocket. For Pangley.'

'Shit,' said Makepeace. She threw the mike on the front seat and ran back towards Thornton's house.

'Dempsey!' she yelled as she ran.

CHAPTER TWENTY-TWO

They saw Spikings and his driver talking to an old man as they pulled into the driveway of Sir Lionel's house. Spikings looked depressed. He regarded them without enthusiasm as they got out of the car. 'Just don't say it,' he told Dempsey gloomily.

'Say what, sir?'

' "I told you so." '

'Nossir. I won't.'

'You get Thornton?'

They both nodded.

'Any trouble?'

'Well, just a bit,' said Dempsey. 'The guy tried to tough it out so Makepeace had to shoot him in the balls.'

'I didn't *mean* to,' protested Makepeace.

Spikings looked at both of them. 'You're not serious,' he said disbelievingly.

'We'll give you a full report later,' she said. 'What about Sir Lionel? Any idea where he might be?'

'No,' sighed Spikings. He turned to the old man. 'This is Mr Pickersgill, Sir Lionel's gardener. We've just searched every inch of the house and grounds together. No sign of either the Judge . . . or Bates.'

'That means he could have taken him anywhere,' said Dempsey. 'Some lonely place on the coast, maybe.'

'I've had an APB out on Sir Lionel since I learned about the missing shotgun. The whole country's on the lookout for him and his Daimler but so far not even a single suspected sighting.'

Makepeace appeared lost in thought. Dempsey noticed and said, 'What is it, princess?'

'I've just remembered something,' she said slowly, with a frown. 'Years ago, on my one and only stay here when I was a schoolgirl, Sarah took me to her favourite spot. It was on the river, not far from here. She liked to go there to get away from her father. It was a very pretty stretch of the river... and it had a boathouse...'

'Ah yes!' exclaimed the gardener. 'I forgot all about that property... Sir Lionel has been meaning to sell it off for years now. He bought it when his wife was alive. He was going to build a cottage there for her...'

Spikings grabbed Makepeace by the arm. 'Let's go!' he cried.

John Bates stood precariously on the chair, the noose now around his neck. He was staring like a hypnotized rabbit at Sir Lionel who was sitting in the same position as before; the shotgun across his knees, the end of the rope in one hand and an old-fashioned, silver pocket watch in the other.

'It's almost time,' he announced, raising his head. 'Guilty or not guilty?' He snapped the watch shut and put it away.

'Guilty... m'Lord...' said Bates in a voice that was little more than a croak.

'Have you anything to say before I pronounce sentence, Mr Bates?'

'No, m'Lord.'

'Then for your crimes I sentence you to be hung by the neck until dead. The sentence will be carried out... *now*.'

'Sir Lionel, don't!'

The Judge turned slowly in his chair. If he was surprised to see Spikings he didn't show it. 'Gordon, my dear old friend,' he said calmly. 'You are just in time to witness the execution of justice. I think you recognize the prisoner in the dock.'

Spikings entered the boathouse, moving very slowly. Dempsey and Makepeace followed him. 'You're making a mistake, Sir Lionel,' said Spikings. 'A terrible mistake.'

'I don't think so, Gordon. And please don't any of you come a step closer.' He raised the shotgun with his free hand and pointed it at them. They froze.

Spikings said, 'Put the gun down, Sir Lionel. That man isn't the one who killed your daughter. We've got him back in London . . .'

Sir Lionel shook his head sadly. 'Bates *is* the one, Gordon. He has admitted it himself. And he must pay the price. An eye for an eye, my dear Gordon, a tooth for a tooth. But the law has gone soft, as you well know, and I know, therefore I have no choice but to execute justice myself.'

'Sir Lionel!' cried Makepeace. 'It's me, Harriet. You know me. I was Sarah's friend. Her best friend. I wouldn't lie to you about this. Bates did not rape and murder Sarah. We just arrested the man who did. He confessed it on his way to hospital. And I promise his punishment has already begun. He'll never rape anyone again . . .'

'I'll second that,' said Dempsey.

'The truth has become a blur,' intoned Sir Lionel. 'Death is the only certainty.'

'*Bates* – did you kill Sarah Hackett?' cried Spikings.

John Bates, his face twisted with anguish, said haltingly, 'Yes . . . I did . . . I killed her . . .'

'See!' said Sir Lionel in triumph.

'Don't be a fool, Bates!' yelled Spikings. 'Your life depends on your answer. Tell the truth! Did you kill Sarah Hackett?'

Bates looked at Sir Lionel and then back at Spikings. 'No . . .' he gasped. 'But I killed my mum . . .'

'No you didn't!' cried Makepeace. 'She's alive! She has a fractured skull but she's going to be all right. And she's made a statement in hospital saying what happened. You're in the clear . . .'

'She's alive . . .?' said Bates.

'Yes!' confirmed Spikings. 'Now tell the Judge again the truth. That you didn't kill his daughter!'

'I'm not guilty, m'Lord,' said Bates. 'That's the truth . . .'

'The truth is a blur . . .' repeated Sir Lionel and tugged sharply on the rope. The chair was pulled from under Bates and he dropped through the square in the floor. The rope went taut and he started to kick and twist convulsively.

Dempsey drew his gun faster than he'd ever done before in his life. The .44 boomed, the sound bouncing off the walls of the boathouse. The rope parted just a foot above Bates' head and he vanished through the hole. There was a loud splash from below.

Dempsey was already running for the door while the echoes of his gunshot continued to fill the boathouse. He tore off his jacket as he ran. Makepeace hesitated for a moment then followed him.

Spikings walked over to Sir Lionel and took the shotgun from his hand. Sir Lionel looked up at him blankly. His wig had tilted to one side and his blue eyes had lost their habitual fierce glare. He now seemed faintly ridiculous. 'It's over, Gordon,' he said sadly.

'Yes sir. It's over.'

The ambulance carrying John Bates sped away down the laneway, its lights flashing and siren screaming. Dempsey, water still dripping from his hair, was sitting on a tree stump, a red blanket around his shoulders. Makepeace, holding his jacket, smiled down at him. 'That was some shooting, cowboy. You saved his life.'

'If he pulls through,' said Dempsey, shivering.

'The ambulance men said he probably would. His neck wasn't broken, that was the important thing.'

Dempsey sneezed. 'Oh hell. I'm catching a cold. I'll be on my back for a week. Colds always wipe me out.'

'You poor dear.'

'Only thing that ever works is a chest rub. My mother is an expert at that. Uses a special Italian liniment.' He gave Makepeace a sly look. 'Are you any good at rubbing chests?'

'Hopeless, Dempsey. But I'll tell you what I will do for you . . .'

'Yeah?' he said eagerly.

'I'll call your mother and tell her you're not well. Perhaps she'll hop on a plane and come over to look after her sick little boy.'

'Gee, thanks,' he said sourly. And sneezed again.

In the rear of Spikings' car Sir Lionel sat slumped like a puppet whose strings had been cut. His face was grey and he seemed to have aged years in the past few minutes.

Spikings regarded him with concerned eyes. 'I'm so sorry about all this, sir.' He paused, then added softly, 'I've got to take you in.'

Sir Lionel nodded. 'Of course you do, Gordon,' he said in a tired voice. 'Of course you do.' He turned and stared out the window. 'Went off the rails a bit, didn't I?'

'Nothing that a good brief won't be able to fix – but I'd reckon on being put out to grass – if you know what I mean, sir.'

'Doesn't matter what happens to me now. Won't bring Sarah back . . . that's the pity of it.' He turned to Spikings. 'You say you've got the man who really killed her?'

'Yes. He's in hospital. Not in very good condition by all accounts – Makepeace shot him. His name is Thornton.'

Sir Lionel frowned. 'Thornton? That name rings a bell.'

'Yes, sir,' said Spikings. 'You sent his brother down for ten years a couple of months ago.'

'What?'

Spikings sighed. 'My deputy, Chas Jarvis, gave me the full story over the radio a short time ago. Thornton confessed everything before they put him under for surgery – he used to work as a minder for his brother Leroy. Leroy Thornton . . .'

'Yes . . . I remember now,' said Sir Lionel slowly. 'He was that black pimp . . . operating in Soho. He threw acid over one of his girls. She gave evidence against him in retaliation . . . it was an open-and-shut case. I gave him the maximum sentence.'

'And I don't blame you, sir. But his brother, this William Thornton, decided to get revenge. He started checking up on you. And found out about Sarah . . .'

'Oh no!' It was a cry of the deepest despair.

'I'm afraid so, sir. He got to know her every movement. Yesterday he decided to strike. He followed her onto the train. No one noticed him because he was wearing the uniform of a British Rail guard. He'd got it off a cousin of his who actually does work for British Rail . . .'

Sir Lionel buried his face in his hands. 'It was my fault then?' he moaned. 'Sarah died because of me!'

Spikings gripped his shoulder. He felt helpless. 'You can't blame yourself, sir. Really you can't.' Then he leaned forward and said to his driver. 'Okay. Let's get moving.'

As Dempsey and Makepeace watched Spikings' car move off Dempsey said, 'I kind of feel sorry for the old guy.'

'I feel more sorry for Sarah,' said Makepeace sombrely, then she shook herself – as if shaking away unwanted memories – and said with forced cheerfulness, 'You feel dry enough yet to eat lunch? My treat – if you promise not to mention the word "hamburger" . . .'

'Lady, you got yourself a deal.' He stood up and removed the blanket. She handed him his dry jacket and he put it on.

As they walked towards the car he said, 'Can I have a hot dog?'

All Futura Books are available at your bookshop or newsagent, or can be ordered from the following address: Futura Books, Cash Sales Department, P.O. Box 11, Falmouth, Cornwall.

Please send cheque or postal order (no currency), and allow 55p for postage and packing for the first book plus 22p for the second book and 14p for each additional book ordered up to a maximum charge of £1.75 in U.K.

Customers in Eire and B.F.P.O. please allow 55p for the first book, 22p for the second book plus 14p per copy for the next 7 books, thereafter 8p per book.

Overseas customers please allow £1 for postage and packing for the first book and 25p per copy for each additional book.